ABOUT THE AUTHOR

William Mayne set out to write books at the age of eight, and about twenty years later won a Carnegie Medal. *Cradlefasts* follows on from *Earthfasts*. Both are set in the part of Yorkshire where the author has lived for many years.

Occasionally he gets the piano out and tries a bit of music writing. Much more often he bakes bread and eats that. Quite a lot of the time he is working out new computer programs for some local schools. Always he is waiting for new ideas for stories. But it is a long time since he was eight and knew how to

Other titles in Signature

Earthfasts
William Mayne

Foundling
June Oldham

Hauntings
Susan Price

Waterbound
Jane Stemp

Cradlefasts

William Mayne

Hodder
Children's
Books

a division of Hodder Headline plc

First published in Great Britain in 1995
by Hodder Children's Books

A Catalogue record for this title is available
from the British Library

ISBN 0 340 65126 1

Typeset by Avon Dataset Ltd, Bidford-on-Avon, B50 4JH

Printed and bound in Great Britain by
Cox & Wyman Ltd, Reading, Berks

Hodder Children's Books
a division of Hodder Headline plc
338 Euston Road
London NW1 3BH

For Catherine and Lulu

First End

Another summer was pushing through the flowers of spring. Martin Malpass said his clerical dog-collar was beginning to stick to his neck. He wound down the driver's window of the Mini and opened the passenger door for Keith Heseltine to get in. They were going to Swang Farm to settle something down, picking up David Wix on the way.

Keith tipped the seat forward and climbed into the back. He felt like a lobster in a pot, several knees to each leg, all elbows, and not wanting to be here, not wanting to remember everything about the summer of the year before.

'David can sit in front,' he said. His hands felt hot and sticky. One day, in that last summer, they had been cold and sticky.

'Mind the box,' said Martin Malpass. 'On the floor behind my seat. It's very little.'

The box was neatly made of wood, with the top shaped to a shallow and elongated dome, like a tea-caddy. Keith put a hand under its top edge and felt the weight. It was not much, but it was more solid than he expected.

All at once he remembered how the sense of cold sweat had run up his arms and somehow left a taste above his teeth, a tang in his throat, not quite a flavour but using those senses.

He fished out a book from under him, because that was giving him real, but ordinary, discomfort here and now.

'I marked the place,' said Martin Malpass. Keith opened the book to half a page of print. 'That's all they provide,' said Martin Malpass. 'I'll pad it out.'

Then they were whizzing across the traffic of Garebrough and into the road behind the Monks' Infirmary, and on to the Health Centre. David was waiting outside his house next door, carrying another, much smaller box. There was careful hand-lettering on its cardboard side.

Before he got into the car he looked back towards his house and gave a little wave.

He got in. He settled his box on his lap.

'Bit more room with only two of you,' said Martin Malpass. 'When was it, eighteen months ago, I gave you a lift to the bowling alley? Middlesbrough Bowlorama.'

David turned his head and looked at Keith and the little wooden box. Keith understood fully what David meant, and how that first journey had been the beginning and cause of this one; and that there had been no way of knowing.

'And nearly a year since the christening,' said Martin Malpass. 'Frank wanted to wait until the flowers were out.'

No one spoke again until they had crossed Jingle Beck at its hairpin bridge and turned off to Swang Farm. The track was bordered golden with dandelions, etched with daisies, tall grass in the middle streaked with tractor oils. It was also rotten with potholes, and here and there summer's water had ponded from wall to wall, with a stony gutter under it out of sight.

'Don't talk,' said Martin Malpass. 'You'll bite your tongue. It's very good and kind of you to come, I want you to know.'

Without saying a word Keith bit his tongue. Or the thought hurt and his eyes watered. David stroked the little box he had brought. The Mini bit a stone with its little wheels and sprayed its windscreen with dazzling mud.

No one would understand this, Keith thought. Sitting in a car

2

like any sort of people, four of us, no one else knowing that what we are doing or feeling about it hurts more than logic can cause. He held back a lump in his throat.

At Swang they drove on to smooth grass, and waited a moment. Keith was short of breath.

'There *isn't* anyone else,' said David, answering Martin Malpass at last.

'Us and Frank Watson and Eileen,' said Keith. 'And Nellie Jack John.'

'And,' said David, remembering something else; but he did not continue his sentence.

We were there, Keith thought, but could not say, that flavour again filling his head.

'Here's Frank,' said Martin Malpass.

Frank Watson came out of the front door of Swang Farm. That door was rarely used, and opened stiffly. Dust fell off the wall above and on to his best black suit. Eileen Watson followed him, fanning dust from her face.

'Frank,' said Martin Malpass, shaking hands with Frank, and then with Eileen, now brushing Frank.

Nellie Jack John came out next with a great deal of noise. He had his regimental uniform on, and was carrying himself stiffly, and beating out a slow rhythm on his drum. He had two original polished regimental drumsticks, black and glinting in the sunlight.

'I hadn't expected that music, John Cherry,' said Martin Malpass, using his official name. 'But it's right, I dare say.'

'Happen,' said Nellie Jack John. 'But a bit of drumming went down well, see-est-ta, time gone by; and this is t'reet pattern for t'do. By Gow, it's a time syne last I donned this gear, and I've brossened. I can hardlins walk.' He had grown taller and broader, he meant, after a year and more at Swang, and the uniform was tight.

It had fitted him when he was a soldier lad, two hundred and

3

more years ago, before he walked through into the present, beating that drum with its sticks, and being found by David and Keith.

Martin Malpass tipped the seat of the Mini forward and brought out the box from behind it.

'I'll take yon,' said Frank, holding out his hands.

'We'll join of it,' said Eileen. 'Eh, Frank?'

'Aye,' said Frank, lowering the box to the level of Eileen's hands. 'It's round in this garden.'

He and Eileen led the way, past the side of the house, through a small and straggly orchard, to a door in a high wall.

Nellie Jack John walked after them, strictly and quietly touching drumsticks to drumhead, setting the pace at which everyone walked, as he had been trained to do centuries ago.

Frank and Eileen passed through the door. Nellie Jack John went through, and the wall swallowed the impact of the drumsticks. Martin Malpass, holding his book, went next, and turned to wait for Keith and David.

Before they got through there was a whistle in the garden beyond, Frank urgently calling a dog to order. Keith was looking at David, so he did not see what dog brushed against him on its way through. There were two, he thought.

David was looking at Martin Malpass, and then at the ground. Keith had thought David would not go through the doorway. But he now smiled, and went through readily.

'It's all right,' he said.

'What does he want with dogs here?' said Keith.

'Oh, Keith,' said David. 'Dogs!'

Of course, Keith remembered. Something else lived at Swang Farm, besides the people and the animals; and that something would want to be here, now, today.

The walled garden was full of the flowers that Frank had waited for, the last daffodils, first bluebells, white jonquils, stalky red and yellow tulips, a spire of larkspur beginning to build, a loop of foxglove ready to rise, and pansies like grass underfoot.

In one place this jewelled turf had been lifted and a hole dug amongst the stones of the country.

'It was a favourite spot,' Eileen was saying, among other things, embarrassed by something Frank had done.

'Of course we had to tell it,' said Frank.

'Oh, well, Frank,' said Eileen. There were things she refused to believe in, she said, 'Especially at a sort of church service.'

Frank got himself down on his knees. Eileen dusted her knees first, and then knelt beside him on the turf. They both held the small wooden box. Frank put an arm round Eileen's shoulders.

Martin Malpass looked at Nellie Jack John. Nellie Jack John looked back, ready for this signal. He rounded off his soft exact tattoo, and put the tips of the sticks level with his chin, according to the official drill, and then rested them down again.

'Dear and heavenly Father,' said Martin Malpass, 'we are here today to offer thanks and prayers for the life, the short life, of Clare, or Donna, Rattray.'

But no one had wanted her, Keith was thinking, his thoughts drowning out the words. She was not easy to want, and hard to like. The garden began to smear round him, and he knew it must be rain on his cheek. Or his tongue was bitten; but that was not the reason. He looked round for help, because there was no rain. David had turned another way, Eileen was bowed over the box, Frank was blowing his nose on a red handkerchief, and the drum was sounding plip, plip, though Nellie Jack John continued upright as a soldier, drumsticks at rest.

I am not alone, Keith thought, and a warm-cold thing ran across his jaw, down his neck, and into his shirt collar.

Martin Malpass's voice crumbled in his throat. There was a gap of words in the order of service for the interment of cremated remains. But a blackbird sang, and then said pick, pick, pick, at something it did not like in the flowery grass.

Martin Malpass continued his words. It is what they are for, Keith thought. They are to make things continue. They are there to tell us what we did and what others did, so that we know what to do next. Unless we hear them we do not know these things very well.

'I will lift up mine eyes to the hills,' said Martin Malpass. Once more Keith's sky cleared, and the hills all about Swang were distinct again too. 'From whence cometh my help.'

Keith rubbed his chin dry.

Then the wooden box like a tea-caddy was in the hole, and Frank wanted to tuck it in with earth.

'She'll want happing up,' he explained.

'There's this,' said David, kneeling to put his little box into the grave too. 'Hers, I reckon. The mouse and his tail and his key. Nothing was her fault. How could it be?'

'She'll need luck,' said Nellie Jack John. He was pulling at his neck-cloth and reaching down under his shirt. He hauled out a string from round his neck. He had to take off his uniform hat to get the string over his head.

'Miners carry a luck-stone on a bit of band,' he went on, swinging the string. The stone was a small one, water-smooth from a beck, bored through by nature. 'It's for thee, tatty-heid;' he told the grave. He wrapped the stone in its own string and laid it in the ground. 'See-est-ta,' he said. He stood up and replaced his headgear.

Keith had his hand in his jacket pocket. 'This is useless,' he said.

'No,' said Martin Malpass. 'It is the continuation of your giving. Your gift transfers to eternity.'

'She would have sucked her face dirty,' said Keith. 'But I got it for her too late to give it to her and kept it ever since.'

David understood. He knew about bars of chocolate. There was no need to explain. Keith laid the package beside the box that held Clare.

'She would have,' said Eileen. 'And everywhere, covers and wall and hair and glasses.'

Frank covered the gifts with earth.

'The only time I met her,' said Martin Malpass, 'up here at Swang, I thought she did not fight to stay alive, but only to be herself while life lasted. I feel she is still very much alive in the eternal sense, in spite of her few years. What was her age? Does anyone know?'

'Today,' said David at once, and very easily. 'Eight years, nine months, a week, and two days, just short of three hours. She died when she was seven years, eleven months, two weeks, six days less three hours.'

'So it's all right,' said Keith, knowing that something had settled in David if he could talk in public about a certain day and time.

'It's been getting all right,' said David.

'I've yet to say the Blessing,' said Martin Malpass. 'To round it off.'

'Then it will all be perfectly all right,' said David. 'We just had to do this.'

'Not so loud on blessings,' said Frank. 'Just us, and the little one. You heard the blackbird.'

Then Keith understood about calling the dog, and how the whistle had been answered, though the dog had been chained up and not come; and why Eileen had been a little cross with Frank.

Martin Malpass said the Blessing, and the service was over.

'And Christ receive thy soul,' said Nellie Jack John. 'That's t'first end on't, anyroad, for t'scallibrat.'

Frank was filling the grave, looking down tenderly. Martin Malpass helped Eileen up.

'I never had one of my own, and never thought to bury one,' she

7

said. 'But she could never have come to anything, and this is peace for her. Well, I do hope that is right.'

'As right as possible,' said Martin Malpass.

'I've to doff this gear,' said Nellie Jack John, 'and get mucking out. Cows won't wait.'

'There's a bit of tea on the table in the house,' said Eileen. 'It's a funeral, so it's right, if you'll come in, Mr Malpass, and you three lads. Muck out after, Nellie.'

The blackbird flung itself from a lilac bush into the air, scolding as it went. The branch it left swung wildly, much more than the weight or departure of the bird could have caused.

'It's the boggart,' said Frank. 'Begging pardon to say it, vicar. No one tek no gaum. He had to be in on the job, but his mind's straight off it now it's owered with.'

'That isn't it,' said David, shading his eyes against more than the sun. 'That's a little one in the tree. The big one's on the wall top. They're playing. I can see them, streaky and dazzling, quite plainly.'

'Laiking?' said Eileen. 'Two of them, Frank?'

'Belike,' said Frank . . .

I

'Hellish,' said Nellie Jack John, very pleased with himself. 'I've gitten a right swing on yon.'

The black ball swayed down the woodwork. A good shot is a good shot, but this one had too much muscle behind it.

David shook his head in the noise of Middlesbrough Bowlorama. His bowl finished its underfloor return journey, rose up the lift and appeared on the rack at the head of the alley.

'It'll be a strike,' said Nellie Jack John. 'By, I do like laiking at skittles. It beats all.'

'Listen,' said David, who could see what was going wrong down the alley, 'we aren't with you.'

'We don't know you,' said Keith.

'What for?' asked Nellie Jack John, standing frozen after his throw. 'Because you're beat?' He was sure he would knock all the pins down. 'You ken me.'

The bowl was swinging from side to side now, and then began hitting the walls of the alley, left side, right side. David looked away, watching from the corner of his eye. Keith shook his head.

'It'll bunch 'em all down,' Nellie Jack John was saying.

'Will it, heck as like,' said Keith.

The bowl jumped the barrier, collided with the bowl of a neighbouring serious game, and between them they knocked down five pins. Then the neighbouring bowl came out from among its pins, jumped the barrier into Nellie Jack John's alley and scored a strike.

The players next door complained at once, because their shot had been spoilt, their electronic scoreboard was now set wrong, and their bowl was being recovered by the wrong lift. They came to protest. Nellie Jack John, brought up in the army, was ready for a scrap. Right and wrong did not matter; the challenge was enough.

'Give up,' said Keith.

The girl at the shoe-counter came out from her place. Her name seemed to be Billy, printed on the lapel of her coat. She had yellow hair in a frizzy and expanded back-combed style. 'Leave it out,' she said, being a few years older than any of the boys involved. Her scent had been strong enough to make Keith sneeze when he went for shoes.

'I thowt it were a good 'un,' said Nellie Jack John. 'It jumped out of it furrow, I weren't to know.'

'It's his first time,' said David.

'It should be his last,' said the lad from the next alley. 'And thrown out and all.'

Keith was expecting trouble and picked up his coat. He saw that David was ready to sort things out by applying sense, but that the best sense was not to be there at all.

'He doesn't know his strength,' David was saying.

But the shoe-counter girl, Billy, could see that Nellie Jack John was not afraid of trouble, and that the other lad would think a fight as much fun as bowling. She looked round.

'Donna,' she called out loudly. Everyone now thought that some extra large woman bouncer would turn up and restore order.

Donna turned out to be a little girl, who looked out from the other side of the counter and knew what to do. She reached out a small hand, and pressed the button of a bell. She was pleased with the rattly singing that cut across the rumbling undergrowth of bowls, the grind of the lifts, the click of bowls, the scatter of skittles, and the canopy of music. She went down out of sight again.

'Not meant to be here, the little rat,' said Billy.

'Well,' said the lad from the next alley, recovering his bowl from the lift, 'We'll be out of time to finish if we don't get back, eh?'

'Tell the manager when he lands,' said the shoe-counter girl. 'We get some rows here, I can't stop them, can I?'

'So side up, Nellie Jack John,' said Keith. 'And calm down.'

'You don't want to sleep in the lock-up,' said Billy. 'Do you?' She went back to her counter, where people were waiting for shoes.

Nellie Jack John stared at her, and shook his head. 'Happen not,' he said. 'You get brayed, after.' He meant beaten.

The manager came along and had a look. There was nothing to see. The lads next door were happy to recover their bowl and give Nellie Jack John's back to him.

'It was his first time,' said David.

'It can always be the last,' said the manager, and left them all arranging a match between the two alleys.

'It's not just all shove,' the lads next door were telling Nellie Jack John, showing him how to stand and how to hold. 'You have to walk down with it, just with your eyes, mind.'

The two alleys closed at about the same time, and the boys went together for drinks and crisps.

'No ale?' said Nellie Jack John. He had been used to ale when he had been a drummer boy in a war against Scotland.

'It was a time-warp,' David explained. No one had difficulty with time-warps or understanding that Nellie Jack John could be 268 years old and lost for most of that time in a secret passage under the castle at Garebrough. People could accept what they were told without being forced to believe it.

'John Cherry, his right name,' said David, in a one-sided introduction. Nellie Jack John turned his head away and looked at the shoe-counter girl.

'Heard of him,' said one of the lads, looking away himself, Middlesbrough style. 'That's him, then?'

There was another time-warp now while they waited for another alley to become free for a joint game. The one they came to was in front of the shoe-counter again.

'Look, it's right,' said David, paying for it. 'We'll get picked up before the time-out and you can finish it. My dad's coming and then we have to get back straight away.'

His father came looking for them about half-way through the match. David was setting up a critical shot.

'Dr Wix is here,' Nellie Jack John called. David did not turn his head, but Keith looked back and put a finger to his lips.

David nearly had a strike, the tenth pin rocking like a milk bottle, and then deciding to stay upright, and changing its mind and tumbling.

'Beat that,' said David. But he and Keith and Nellie Jack John had to abandon the game there. Nellie Jack John took his shoes and David's to the counter and handed them in. Keith had a problem with a knot left by an earlier hirer, and then took his along.

'Come on, Nellie, said Keith, because Nellie Jack John was still there, looking hard at the girl, Billy. However, the girl was looking at Keith, and at Dr Wix. She was also putting a hand on her child, lying beside her on two chairs, partly covered with a spread of dark fur.

'You'll be from Garebrough,' said Billy.

'Yes,' said Keith. 'Why?'

'Nowt,' said Billy, running a hand through her hair. 'Haven't been there in a bit, have we, Donna?'

The little girl blinked and picked her nose. Her glasses were greasy.

'Is it yours?' asked Nellie Jack John.

'That?' said Billy. 'Just looking after it for a friend, eh, Donna?'

'Mams,' said the child, opening her eyes wide and blinking, clutching a worn furry toy.

Dr Wix was wanting to leave. Keith dragged Nellie Jack John away.

'She's the spit of our Kath, is that Billy,' said Nellie Jack John, looking back all the way to the doors. 'Bar she hasn't gitten t'ringlets off quite right.'

Bitter weather outside got into his mouth.

Because of the time-warp his Kath was two and a half hundred years ago. But he had to put his dreams somewhere.

Dr Wix's car smelt faintly of ether. It had, too, the light fresh scent of Sister Mackenzie, the nurse at the Health Centre, who was in the front seat.

'Just about room in the back for three sturdy lads,' said Dr Wix.

'There wasn't any when we came,' said David. They had come in Martin Malpass's Mini, folded and cooped up small. Martin Malpass had been to a convenient church meeting, and Dr Wix and Sister Mackenzie to an inconvenient one about the district accident emergency schedules. Sister Mackenzie had arranged the taking to Middlesbrough and fetching back, as if they were patients being allocated ambulances.

'There are buses,' Keith was telling Nellie Jack John. 'But she'll be fixed up. The town girls are.'

'I could walk on some night,' said Nellie Jack John. 'By, she's another clipper.'

'What's taken your fancy this weather?' Sister Mackenzie asked.

'The girl who gives out shoes,' David told her.

'She does baby-sitting as well,' said Keith.

'She was sorting out fights,' said David. 'Which we didn't have.'

'I were ready,' said Nellie Jack John. 'Right and ready. That would have shown that lass.'

The first snows of a long winter were dodging the headlights before Keith was dropped off at his house. He saw the hill tops speckled with flakes, but roofs and roads were still dry. Only the castle tower held a reflected street-lamp gleam on battlement and parapet.

II

On a very cold Saturday late in the following March there were dirty fingernails of ice between the cobbles of the market place. In Finkle Street snow was lying like a geological deposit, full of fossil snowflakes and yellow marks where dogs had left each other freeze-dried messages – some for Santa Claus perhaps – because the snow had been here since the middle of December. The surface of Victoria Road was dry and white with salt. Part way along it the water board had abandoned a hole in the pavement and left a flashing light.

Keith walked through and past them all on the way to visit David, if David happened to be in. He wore an old shooting coat of his father's.

'I might get mucky,' he had told his mother.

'It'll wash,' she said. 'Like the rest of your clothes.'

At David's house he went into the back yard, beyond the Health Centre, saw a light, clicked up the sneck of the back door, and looked in. David was at home, and both in and out.

Dr Wix was in the back room with a stack of paperwork, and Sister Mackenzie from the Health Centre was typing letters for him.

'Come in,' said Dr Wix. 'But if you want David he's up in his shed. He'll tell you why, but you won't need to be told when you get close.'

Zapata zapata pling, went the typewriter, and Sister Mackenzie looked up with a smile between lines.

Heat lifted visibly out of the shed door when Keith went up there and opened it. David had a gas-fire going on a low setting. The shed was not very warm with the door shut. It was quite unheated with the door open.

David too was doing paperwork, sorting something like a stack of letters still in their envelopes, or in small packets. 'Come in if you can bear it,' he said. 'It's smelly and cold.'

'I can just thole it,' said Keith, coughing a little, because the smell was strong.

'It's not worth changing, or getting too warm,' said David. 'I don't want to tramp the stink into the house. I've to go back to Swang and milk tonight, and then there's tomorrow morning, but I get the rest of the day off. You'd better come up in the afternoon, tomorrow.'

'It's all clean muck,' said Keith.

'It goes on all the year round,' said David. 'That's what. You don't realise until you have to do it every day, even if you think you know. It's the silage I don't care for. Nellie Jack John doesn't like it either. Too modern, he says.'

David was doing a fortnight's work experience at Swang Farm with Frank Watson, where Nellie Jack John was a full-time hand. He knew all the old ways of farming, and with Frank was not learning the very newest.

'That's why I didn't choose farming,' said Keith. 'Frank Watson isn't my only relative in that job, so I knew what it was like.'

'Perfectly good logic,' said David. 'And I didn't choose school teaching because I know all these people being educated. In fact they've tried it on me. So what do you smell of?'

Keith had finished his first week's work experience at the primary school. 'Nothing changes,' he said. 'You know those dinners – I can still taste them. How do they make them so mean? I'd rather have silage.'

'Stick to silage for all your needs,' said David. 'I wasn't at primary school much, remember. I went to Barnard Castle when I stopped being an infant, and when I came back it was into big school.'

'I don't think I'll go for teaching,' said Keith. 'The chalk breaks and they laugh, and there's an outbreak of head-lice. Another week will be plenty. I don't think I like it. The kids don't call me Sir, or even Mister, but Keith.'

'The cows just call me Moo,' said David. 'Another week will do for me too. I like it, but it isn't where I'm going. It's one of those things you can get more feel about by watching, not doing.'

'What are you doing now?' said Keith. 'Is it Frank's accounts, or something?'

David leafed through the heap. 'Look,' he said, drawing a folded paper out of an envelope. Keith opened it out. it was a letter. He saw the writing of Dr Wix, but large and careful.

'Read it,' said David. 'It's how he used to be. I'd sort of forgotten.'

'Who is it to?' Keith asked, not reading any words so far. 'Why would he write to you? You live here.'

'When I was away at school in Barnard Castle,' said David. 'You ugly idiot.' This was a perfectly friendly remark. 'When I was at school here I saw him every day.' He kicked the gas-fire to bring it to order. 'I saw them both.'

A little silence followed David's words. This was the first time he had ever mentioned his mother. Only the gas-fire popped, finding the frosty air or the kick indigestible. There was nothing for Keith to say about Mrs Wix. He could not tell whether he remembered her or not.

The letter began, 'Dearest Davy,'.

'Davy,' said Keith. 'I didn't . . .'

'You don't,' said David, flatly. 'Not because you're an ugly idiot, but it's private speech. You didn't see that bit.'

'No,' said Keith. 'I wouldn't think of you as that, only as a ham-fisted bucket of worms.'

'You'll be a scientist yet,' said David. 'Read the rest, if you like.'

I should like your advice on the following problem, the letter went on. *One of my patients, a Mr Bazangalong, of Octopus Street, has presented me with an interesting complaint. He was born with two heads, which he now carries everywhere in an attaché case, even when swimming and especially when having his hair cut. One of the heads says it has toothache, and the other says it is going bald. He would like both these conditions to be cured, but the difficulty is that neither head will have anything to do with the other and says it is a stranger. So if he experiences toothache he goes to the dentist, which means, as you know, that the tooth stops hurting at once. Since the other one will not report, he can't tell which head has to have the drill and the extraction and pink polishing. And as for the baldness, both heads say it's the other one, and they don't care, and neither of them will take the baldness medicine. Or the pink hair-polish. Mr Bazangalong cares very much, and says his social life is a heap of ruins, but he can't get either head to swallow the cure. What do you suggest?*

We shall come over on Saturday morning after surgery hours. Mummy is bringing Matron some clothes for you (I was astonished to hear you had none!). I have measured her again and she is another inch further round the middle (Mummy, I mean, not Matron!).

Love, Dad. Mummy sends a million of love. She is writing a separate letter.

'I don't know Octopus Street,' said Keith. 'I read to the end. Of the letter.'

'That's right,' said David. 'But you know he isn't like that any more, and perhaps it's because I'm not either.'

'It all changed,' said Keith. 'When your . . .'

'And,' said David, riding over Keith's words, 'I've been working up at Swang with Nellie Jack John, scaling and that—'

18

'Scaling?' said Keith, wondering why he did not know this farming word when he was related to Frank and David was not. 'You're using technical words on purpose.'

'We dump heaps of muck on the field and then go round and scale them, spread them about,' said David. 'And he's lost both his parents a long time ago and got used to it, so it isn't difficult for him. It's difficult for me. Every time it gets easier it gets more difficult too.'

'Nellie Jack John has had longer,' said Keith. 'From the eighteenth century.' He had been a drummer boy come to this century with only his memories, out on the hillside, beating a drum, smiling, while down in the town below the church bells had been shimmering to the close of their peal. He had brought with him a sort of time-candle, or it had brought him across the two centuries.

'Not really,' said David.

'Well, he hasn't had longer in himself,' Keith admitted, recalling the candle. Time-warps get you there without the intervening time.

However, he was thinking that he was the ugly idiot friend of the ham-faced bucket of worms and ought to have shared thoughts with David first.

But perhaps David was only changing into his future self, not away from those who knew him, only unknown until he got there.

'But I can't mention it to him,' said David, meaning his father, not Nellie Jack John. Then he thought that conversation was over and changed the subject again. 'It's cold,' he said. 'But I've to stop out here until I'm sent for to Swang, and that depends what mood the pig's in.'

'But the telephone's in the house,' said Keith. 'Oh, they'll come and tell you.'

'There's other ways,' said David.

Half an hour later Keith said, 'Thunder,' hearing a muffled rumpus outside. 'No, it'll be the quarry blasting off. No it can't be, it's closed.'

'Quiet,' said David, getting up, opening the door, and going out. The gas-fire cowered against the attack of winter that came in. 'Nellie Jack John is calling me. He won't use the telephone.'

The noise was clearer outdoors. It was a message from a drum, pulsing through still air, then falling silent.

'I'll have to be off,' David went on. 'I'll just give him a shout back.' He had brought a bugle out with him. He licked his lips, put the bugle to them, concentrated for a moment, and sent a vaulting message, like lightning following thunder.

'He's saying nothing back,' said Keith, listening.

'Distance,' said David. 'It'll take fifteen seconds to get there, probably via satellite. He'll acknowledge any day now.'

Half a minute later there was an explosion of sound far away, and the transaction was complete.

Sister Mackenzie, however, came out of the Health Centre, wondering what was happening. Dr Wix came out from his house enquiringly too, then offered to take David along to Swang.

'I'll cycle to the lane end and then drive,' said David. 'Frank's left a Land-Rover there for me.'

Before he left he hid away the bundle of letters, turned the gas out, put on a mucky coat, a cowman's hat, and encrusted gumboots.

David was getting his bicycle from the coal-shed. Another bicycle was leaning down on it.

'It belongs to Sister Mackenzie,' said David. 'I'll have to bring it out first. Hang on to Dulcinea,' He gave Keith Sister Mackenzie's crafty-looking mountain bike to hold. 'She cycles in the Alps and places. Up Norway and down Sweden.'

'Dynamo hub,' said Keith, sizing up the machine. 'Automatic gears. I could come on up to Swang with you if—'

'Ask her,' said David.

III

At the lane to Swang they put both bikes on the back of the Land-Rover pick-up. David turned the key, then started the engine, and the diesel smoke thudded out in a cloud.

'Not bad from clap-cold,' said David. 'And the oldest Land-Rover in the world. Nothing works.'

'My door won't fasten,' said Keith.

'Typical – just hold it,' said David, now sitting tense and upright, having to get the first actions right, with clutch down, gear rammed in, handbrake off, blip of the throttle, and the wheel under his hands stiff and slim as ice. 'Hold the gear-lever in too, and I'll be able to steer.'

The Land-Rover moved forward. 'It's the ruts,' said David, when there was a thump and a bump and the steering-wheel wanted to turn by itself. There was no heater. The windscreen frosted over with breath. But they were on the track and going.

'Even changing gear,' said David. 'Well,' he added a little later, after some noises, 'nearly. We're back where we started with the gearbox. Maybe it's only got one gear left.'

'It's stripped my teeth,' said Keith.

David drove round into the yard, turned round, pretended he had stopped the engine so suddenly on purpose, and switched off. 'It's the only way,' he said. 'There aren't any brakes.'

'It'll make a man of you yet,' said Frank Watson, hunched in an overcoat and a woolly hat. 'Have you brought another fellow to help? I'll pay the same as you get – experience.'

'He gets his own,' said David. 'Teaching.'

'Kids,' said Keith.

'There's farmers and there's scholars,' said Frank. 'That's a fine and fancy hay-making bike, Keith.' But he was not waiting for answers. 'Where's that lad at?'

Nellie Jack John was coming off the hillside above Swang, and into the yard with a milk can. He rinsed it at the pump.

'He's been up on the fell,' said Frank, seeing him. 'Lead mining and that, daft beggar. My dad remembered taking milk to the lead miners on the hill. He was one himself a long time. Weekends and all at the Powderhouse.'

Nellie Jack John said nothing.

'We'll shift the sow first,' said Frank, hearing the nothing. He knew it was a reply.

He had been in with her, digging out a layer of muck to get at the door of the sty, throwing it into a coupe cart. 'This will spread. Noo, get back, Martha, gissie, gissie.' The sow was not happy about a human coming in and digging up her floor. 'Put a bale of straw in the far end, John, and we'll get her in. She'll be better off there when she pigs.'

Martha came out, then went back in the warm again. She trotted out and went to have a word with the dog. The dog was tied up, and the sow had a good sniff from a distance, teasing and walking in a circle just out of reach.

She was satisfied with her new quarters when she got into them. Frank had tipped out some feeding nuts into the straw for her to rummage out.

'She had eight first time,' said Frank. 'She's the insurance pig, but my right one would have had twelve or fifteen, so I lost out.' But he scratched her back and said, 'Eh, Martha.'

Not quite two years before, all the local pigs had vanished and the insurance company had replaced them. The lost pig had been black and white, and Martha was too.

Frank went to milk, switching on lights in the shippon. The three boys emptied the pig hole in the twilight, David and Keith making a mound of dung and straw, Nellie Jack John filling the cart with it as they went.

They talked as they worked. 'Nay, this is easy,' Nellie Jack John said. 'None so hard, anyroad. We have nowt where I come from. Nay, where I came from. Nowt. I ken well I'll not get back yonder. But by, it was hard, and owt you addled you spent and more. It were grand in t'army, yal, you got, and your meat.' He meant ale and food. 'And you'd never to fetch the sheep by, nor get yourself down a lead mine. But I wish I was never into a lead mine, for if I hadn't known how to frame in one I'd niver have gitten in where I did after treasure and that.'

He had gone in as a drummer boy, beating his drum, with two more lads to follow above and help him dig out the treasure. But he had come out two and half centuries out of time.

'I'll not get back, and while I don't want to stop here, I less still want to land back for ever where I came from. And if I missed our Kath, well . . .'

'Another bus along in a minute,' said Keith. 'My dad says.'

'That's t'road on't,' said Nellie Jack John. 'By Gow, this stuff is ram.'

When the stinking cart was full it steamed in darkness. Nellie Jack John switched off the light in the pig hole, and Keith's shadow jumped 180°, because the moon now shone from the other side of him. His moon shadow was darker than his electric one, but his actual light was weaker.

What shall I remember? he wondered. That I am standing in a remote farmyard by a cart of muck and straw, with the moonlight casting a sickly gleam over the smelly stuff? Or can I forget it?

'It's extraordinary and strange and memorable,' said David, being struck by the same objects and events but having a different view. 'It's real and romantic. Look at the steam in the moonlight. It's like a painting. You could pick up the shadow of that gripe standing up on the back, like something solid.'

'Just a muckfork,' said Keith. Nellie Jack John had stabbed it in when the job was over, ready for a day's tipping and scaling.

'Another technical word,' said David. 'You can't just say muckfork.'

'Sometimes,' said Keith, 'you are completely wrong in the head.' And he was touched with jealousy at David's knowing a word that should belong to Keith's own dialect and farming relatives.

'There's many a worse thing,' said Nellie Jack John. 'I's off. I've an errand before the day's done. Tell her I'll be in for my tea.'

'I'll milk with Frank,' said David. 'Pump the pump for me, Keith.'

Keith pumped. A coating of ice in the pump snagged on the piston. Nellie Jack John went into the dairy and came out with the milk can he had been carrying before.

'Shan't be so very long,' he said, and went out of the yard through the far little gate into the farm garden.

David rubbed his sleeves up above his elbows and put his arms under the spouting water.

'I was warm before,' he said, finishing his rinsing and pulling his sleeves down. 'I'll warm again milking in the shippon. Get your sleeves up. I'll just pump for you and then.'

'My thumbs hurt,' said Keith a moment later, the water seeming to fall on him in lumps, hard and cold as ice.

Something came out of the pigsty. This thing was not visible to Keith, but moonlight passing through it was wrinkled, like the light through the warm steam of the cart. David could see the thing itself as a patch of interference.

24

'Boggart,' he said quietly. 'Not so happy.'

Perhaps the boggart had been happy in with the pig. Perhaps it liked the midden smell and warmth. It found the cart, hopped up into it, and began to burrow down. The gripe on the top wobbled and fell over. Keith laughed at that. The boggart looked out from his new home. A sloppy chunk of midden flew out and draped itself on Keith's left shoulder. The smell made his eyes water.

He took the coat off and went in to talk with Eileen.

'They'll be done in an hour,' said Eileen. 'Then wanting their teas, if you like to wait. But David will be working after, foddering and that.'

'Just getting my hands warm,' said Keith. 'Before they drop off.'

'Oh, isn't it wintry?' said Eileen. 'And going on so long and just as bad in town for once.'

'Frank grumbling,' said Keith.

'Take no gaum,' said Eileen. 'He best knows how to do it all without help, so help hinders.'

Keith cycled back down the track with ice forming at the corners of his eyes. He was wondering at having being invited for the next afternoon. Usually he and David came together without arrangement or having to be formal. He's got the wrong head on, he thought, feeling toothache and baldness setting in. Or I have.

The cycle wheels snake-tracked through the crisp centre of the track, where the snow was grimy but untouched. Then he was on the bitter dry road, riding into town as if he had come all the way from Muker or Arkengarthdale.

The road swooped down to the bridge over Jingle Beck, curled over it, and slogged up the other side. Automatic gears meant he did not miss any power strokes. The road swung now away from the valley of the beck, where the road over the moor went straight on. It went level past the derelict quarry, where grits and gravels made their own drifts under the snow, and dropped down into town.

After delivering the bicycle Keith walked down through the evening town in moonlight and lamplight. He thought about his tea, a street or two away, wondering whether he could wait quite so long and whether it wasn't necessary to go into the sweet shop and buy supplies to help him the last two hundred yards. Sweet shops always close last.

Just in case, he was thinking, of a fresh snowfall and being buried. If it doesn't happen now it might tomorrow, and too late for the shop then. His mouth watered without being consulted.

He decided not to make up his mind, but wait and see what happened at the shop door.

A small blue car with curling flames painted across its bonnet and along its sides came down the market place behind him, passed him, and stopped on the hill outside the sweet shop. The driver got out and went to the shop door. She was smoking.

Going for cigarettes, thought Keith, disapproving but not actually caring. But the woman waited at the shop door.

A second later Keith decided he had grown up, and didn't want sweets any more. Out of the shop came four children. They buy sweets, he realised. I don't.

The children were from the primary school. They called out, 'Keith, Keith,' and came to meet him, thumbing out wrapped boiled sweets or unwrapped jelly ones, and making him take them before hurrying away up the market place.

Keith had four sweets, and no way of ever becoming Sir or Mister, or of being of any importance at all. But his mouth had stopped watering for sweets, for ever.

On Monday he was not going to be sure which children they had been.

The little blue car sat by the kerb, its engine trundling, and blue smoke dropping from its exhaust pipe. The driver, in a dark hairy coat looking as if it had been made from a dog, was helping one

26

more child down the two steps of the sweet shop. Keith stood a moment to let them cross the pavement, because the little girl was not able to walk well. She held a bag, presumably of sweets, in one hand, and a soft toy in the other.

She seemed about six years old, with a clamped-down sad mouth in a white face, straight short hair, and wearing big glasses with pink frames, the plastic full of sparkly bits. The mother was helping but impatient, and also telling the child something. Keith had seen her somewhere, but she had seemed younger then, by a long way. He thought she said, 'That's the one. Tell him.'

The little girl shook her head and almost fell down. She dropped the bag of sweets and could not bend to pick it up on the sloping pavement.

Keith picked the bag up for her, and handed it to the mother.

'It's hard for her,' the mother said to Keith. 'You can see that, eh?' Then she said to the child, 'This is Garebrough. You come from here. You know his name. Tell him what I told you.'

Keith was going away, because this was not his conversation, and there was no way it made sense. But the little girl stretched out an arm towards him, and leaned over so that he was holding her weight. She held his jacket and drew herself closer.

The mother was hung about with scent. The little girl smelt different. David had smelt, but rich, not raw, and that was his working clothes. This was a dirty child. I'm not much better, Keith thought, with the stink the boggart threw on me.

The mother was smiling at him. They think I am someone else, Keith decided. But there was no way of speaking, or of leaving. If he walked off the child would fall over. He went closer to the blue car, the mother opened the passenger door, and the child got in very awkwardly, partly because of what was wrong with her legs, and partly because she was holding one side of Keith's jacket with both hands. She had to hold or fall.

27

Then she let go of Keith and stared at him with mud-coloured eyes. She took her bag of sweets in both hands. She shook her head again at some more of her mother's words, which Keith did not catch, and went on looking.

Keith closed the car door. The driver revved up with a tearing noise, and went off round the corner.

At first Keith thought it was another pupil he had not recognised. But at the house door a recollection came back to him. The child had rung the bell at the Bowlorama, and the mother was Billy, the shoe-counter girl. That had been Middlesbrough. But in Garebrough she was a complete stranger. Now she had plain cheeks, a mouth without lipstick, and her hair was not bouffant but tied back, invisible. What didn't she tell me? he wondered. It probably isn't me.

'Tea's just on,' said his father at the door with a policeman, Constable Hunter, when he got home. 'How was Frank?'

'How did you know I'd seen Frank?' said Keith.

'There's detection for you,' said his father. 'The smell of Swang is like no other. You're as ripe as can be, so that's where you were.'

'I went up with David,' said Keith.

'Go round and hang that coat out back,' said his mother from the kitchen. 'Don't bring it in.'

His father went on for a moment at the door, talking to the policeman about a possible break-in at a property he dealt with. 'I'll take a look as soon as I can,' he said. 'There aren't any contents to consider, way up there.'

'I was just thinking of explosives,' said the policeman. 'There. What they say. Folk still looking.'

'Not these last hundred years,' said Mr Heseltine.

'Worse folk about these days, and all,' said Constable Hunter.

Keith had to wait outside the door without his coat until the constable went.

'At least I can come in,' Keith said. 'David finds it easiest to stay outside.'

'Well,' said his mother, 'there's more than one reason for that. But I think it'll work out.'

'We'll see what happens,' said his father. 'And say nothing.'

So they said nothing, and Keith could not ask what was in their minds.

Going to bed later that evening he heard the frost again cracking the roofs. When he had turned out the light he sat for a moment in bed, feet warm, back frozen, and looked at glittering ridges and slates and the curtained glow of windows. Overhead the stars were in full bloom, all colours, like new electric buds in a strange garden.

Below them the hills stretched snowy, the walls clear. Here and there a distant house light sat. On top of one hill overlooking the town a small window glowed.

Nobody lives there, Keith thought, lying down, trying to work out what the light would be, and falling asleep before he did so.

IV

David left a message on the answering machine on Sunday morning while Keith was at chapel.

'Hello, machine, beep to you too,' David said to it. 'Tell Keith that it's clean clothes this afternoon because we're going down to the town, that's all. Don't ring, I'm in the bath.'

Mr Heseltine efficiently reset the machine.

'I'll wear these chapel clothes,' said Keith.

'Anything but what you had on yesterday,' said his mother. 'Not much happening in town on a Sunday afternoon, so stop clean.'

'It's clean weather, frost,' said his father.

David's shed up the yard was warmer today, and smelling only of paint blistered by the gas-fire.

Keith sniffed. 'Makes a change,' he said. 'It's you that needed clean clothes, not me.'

'They're all in the wash,' said David. 'Ready to start again tomorrow. I'm just filling out my notes on the job, so pull up a sock and sit down.'

'If you're going to make jokes,' said Keith, 'try something funny.'

The notes were a record to show that work experience had really been experienced. Keith had written his day by day, without managing to convey his real impressions, or perhaps even knowing them: being thumped by a big girl half his size (and wanting to cry from it); dropping the staffroom biscuit tin and all the

31

biscuits; kicking the football over the wall.

'Monday morning,' said David, 'shovelling. Tuesday, shovelling more you-know-what. Wednesday, another consignment. Cow 278 very prolific.'

'But you're in charge,' said Keith. 'The kids are in charge at my place. They know it all and they take no notice of me if they don't want.'

'Nor do I,' said David. 'Normal.'

'I've forgotten playground games,' said Keith.

'Friday,' said David, 'banished from house. 'Saturday . . . Look, I'll just do this properly and then it's over. Have another letter to read.'

'Mr Bazangalong again?' said Keith.

'Who? Don't tell me,' said David. 'I can't read them. I know they're funny, but they make my eyes water. It must be an allergy makes me feel like I'm going to cry. But I want someone to read them.'

Dear Davy, the next letter ran, *Mrs Clamjamphrey, who lives near the Gallimaufrey Trading Estate, has recently been delivered of twins. This was of course at the Monks' Infirmary, where Mum will soon be. Mum will of course have a human child, judging by her first effort (if you have been attending you will know who that is). But Mrs Clamjamphrey, by using her imagination to the full, had two spaniel puppies, one ginger, the other black with a spotted white belly. One was a dog, and one a bitch, so they are technically dizygotic, from two eggs, not monozygotic, from one egg that divided and produced identical babies. They are both very healthy, so obviously nothing is wrong, and Mrs Clamjamphrey is totally pleased. Her other children are human, and such a trial to her. But the new ones sleep in a basket and are fed on scraps and will be very economical. They are the talk of the Gallimaufrey Trading Estate, and she has refused several offers to sell them. I think the price was too low – she has a mother's pride, after all.*

Your own Mum is another quarter of an inch round the equator. There are definite signs it is going to be an Alsatian. I know you would probably prefer a helicopter, but science is not up to it yet. Also they are so dizzygotic.

Love Dad. Mum is resting at the moment and is writing tomorrow. She says it is good about the Latin, and the vocative of 'me' is 'me' though it doesn't mention it in the book. She means that when we say in English, 'O my', the Latin is 'O me', and when we say 'O my hat', the Latin is, 'O mea titfa'.

Love Dad – I don't mind saying it twice.

David was still writing. Keith was glad. He preferred to say nothing. Like David, he thought, he had a slight allergy and a prickling in the eyes. That was because he knew what had happened afterwards. He folded the letter and put it in its envelope again.

'Funny stuff,' said David, in almost a question.

'Yes,' said Keith. 'He was younger then.'

'That's it,' said David. 'Just check another, will you?' He handed over another envelope, larger and stouter, with a solid thing inside it.

The solid thing was a bar of chocolate, its wrappings untouched, but the shape of it warped in a strange way, perhaps by time. There was a piece of tissue paper that had wrapped something else, but which was now empty. There was a short letter.

Writing this in the middle of surgery. All the patients have spots today, small and large. One little girl has a spot so big she wheels it about in her doll's pram dressed as a clown. Don't eat the chocolate all at once or you might get spots too. Mum says she hopes the tail does not fall off again, it must be so painful. She sends her love and says look after it (the tail she means, but the love too, I'm sure). Now I have a customer with such a severe rash I need a map to show me the way. Don't be a doctor, the diseases are too excitable.

Love, Dad.

'Chocolate,' said Keith, because he had to talk about something and thought a tail might be too private and . . . well, medical families are so talkative about certain things.

'I kept it until the right day,' said David, looking at him. 'Under my pillow, usually. It got soft. There wasn't a right day. They . . . I got lots of it, but I never ate it. It would be like eating . . . people. It wasn't chocolate, you see, but something I could feel, but not an actual eating thing.'

'From them,' said Keith. He laid the letter down. He understood how David was identifying the gift with the giver. Cannibals eat strong enemies to gain strength for themselves.

David looked away, slapped the table hard with his flat hand, 'I've finished my notes,' he said firmly. 'We'll go down into the town.'

He put the letter into its envelope and all the envelopes into a box. He turned out the gas-fire and the frost came back into the shed. There was nothing but frost outside, at head and foot and heart.

'Dad isn't coming today,' said David. 'He's on road call, accidents on the A1.'

'So what are we doing?' Keith asked. But he knew he was being shown more of David's privacy, even before David scarcely answered.

'You tell me,' said David. 'After.' Then he changed the subject to birds, which Nellie Jack John had been teaching him about. 'That's a fieldfare,' he pointed out, in the playing-field beside Victoria Road, going round the water board's repair hole and flashing light, and having to hop back on to the pavement because of some large traffic.

'And that's a return fare,' said Keith, because the large traffic had been a bus from Reeth.

Then they went quite happily along, noting such species as the knock-kneed centenarian, crossing the cobbles in its gaudy plumage, and the white-headed dull gazing blankly into a closed shop.

No one was about on the Brompton Road, except a great nit, or bare-kneed jogger. Keith did not know where he was going. David gave him no help by saying, 'Don't come if you don't want.'

'It's all right,' said Keith, not asking, but ready to trust David. It was clear that David could not say, and that was mysterious and strange, but David was reliable. It was not possible that he would do something embarrassing.

Neither of them was talking now, and that was strained and unnatural. Keith felt for those four sweets from yesterday, to give their jaws something to live for. But they were in another trouser pocket.

The town stretched so far and then stopped. They went out of it. There were fields to one side, the river beyond.

Keith thought back almost a year and a half, to when they had found Nellie Jack John coming out of the ground, walking out of it, beating his drum. This afternoon the next reasonable objective was the ruined Abbey down by the river, the sort of place to continue those ideas. Perhaps David had found something to speculate on; a secret room, Keith thought; the treasure of the . . .

'In here,' said David, going through a small door in a high stone wall.

Keith followed him off the narrow but endless road into a place he had not known about. There was a lumpy lawn, with stones standing in it. They were gravestones, with here and there a table tomb. This was a churchyard, and the church stood to one side of it.

This was far from town, far beyond the point where gardens

changed to fields. Out of the frozen overcast a suffusion of sunshine filled that place only. Keith felt that it must always have its own light, within its own high walls.

'St Agatha's,' said David. 'It was here before they built the new church in town.'

'I'm chapel,' said Keith. But he knew that did not explain his ignorance. 'I didn't know this was here. Why here? Is it a short cut to the Abbey?'

'I don't know,' said David. 'I just wanted someone to come here with me before – well before another person does.'

He knew where he was going in this grassy plot.

'No good bringing anything,' he said. 'In this weather. Technically it isn't any use ever. But people do it. A sort of reverse botanising.'

Keith did not know what David meant at all until he stopped at a stone let into the ground. There was a crust of lacy ice over it. He squatted down and eased the ice away until the lettering showed.

'Elizabeth Wix,' it said, 'July 9th,' with the year, seven years ago, and below that 'and an infant daughter'. The stone itself was fresh and clear, not long carved. David had not brought flowers, the reverse botanising.

'Not long done,' said Keith, because the edges of the letters were crisp, the stone unstained by moss or lichen or tainted by rain. He made no comment, knowing more than he had, reading letters an hour earlier, the reason for showing those letters clear to him, and knowing that David was at last admitting another person, a friend, to his feelings. He did not know what the whole message meant to David.

'Over here,' said David, stepping to the wall and lowering another stone that stood facing it, 'is something not many people see.'

The stone against the wall had lettering on it too. Some of it had weathered, and those words were the same as those on the gravestone itself. But carved later and fresher on that were the words 'David Francis Wix' and David's date of birth, and the date he had been thought dead. The day he had been seen to die.

That had been after Nellie Jack John came from the ground, after he had gone back in, when David had been vaporised by lightning, and his name added to his mother's and sister's.

Keith could remember the inquest on dead David.

He could remember that Dr Wix decided to live in another country.

David had been found again, and the inscription with his name on replaced. But for Nellie Jack John, a very old man at Eskeleth had told them, there had been 'Never an arval, nor priest, nor owt'.

'It's unusual,' said Keith, by David's empty grave, stamping his feet because the cold ground had got into them, not knowing what to say, all his sugary biscuits of thought scattered on the carpet of frost.

'That's nothing,' said David. 'I don't remember being dead. One moment I was on the moor with you, and the next we were in cave and you brought that time-warp candle and we walked out. With Nellie Jack John, without the candle. Today I just wanted someone to come here and prove this is real.' He brushed the stone in the ground with his fingers again.

'Those letters,' said Keith. Then there was a moment when Dr Wix's letters to David and letters inscribed on stone were confused and had to be sorted in their minds and words. Dr Tate at school insisted on such exercises.

'Shut up,' said David at last. 'I know. He isn't like that any more. She isn't here at all, and I'm not there, but this is the eternity-warp chamber. I know that. But are the letters all right? Are they funny? I can't read them, but I want to know. Not these inscriptions but the ones they wrote.'

'They're great,' said Keith. 'Like in a book.'

'The only problem.' said David, 'is that you are an ugly idiot with no sense of humour, so how can you know?'

'Impossible,' said Keith, able to smile now that David valued him again.

'That's all right then,' said David. 'Feeling abnormal is normal for me as well as for you.'

'Definitely,' said Keith.

'When I was little I kept thinking she would speak,' said David. 'Is that possible? Or is it me talking to myself?'

'Talk to yourself and you don't hear so much,' said Keith. 'Somebody else hears you and they hear plenty.'

'You've obviously had a brain transplant,' said David.

'My dad said it,' said Keith.

'We'll go on home and have something to eat,' said David. 'I'll catch you up.'

'I'll get started on cake and that,' said Keith.

David caught him up by the Monks' Infirmary.

'Just remind me,' he said, capering along a raised pavement above Keith. 'What was that curious joke you nearly made about a fieldfare?'

'I'd tell you,' said Keith. 'But it would be un-fare.'

When they came to Dr Wix's house Sister Mackenzie was there, doing paperwork and putting on the kettle. Dr Wix touched her elbow to interrupt what she was saying. David looked away and did not see it. Keith saw, and began to understand what David was not seeing. He understood too why seeing it might be painful for David. His faith and truth were at St Agatha's.

V

Frank Watson at Swang Farm expected David to work through the weekend and go milking on Sunday afternoon. He had even had to work through his first weekend, before work experience really began. David was cheerful about that, happy at it all hours. Now it was his last Saturday afternoon, and Frank had come into town and dropped him off for a while, expecting to be met in the market place at three o'clock. Milking was to follow, David said, at Keith's door.

Keith had finished his work experience last Friday afternoon at half past three. He had finished with children too, coming away without gaining much. 'The generation gap already showing,' he told his mother.

From that they were now working out how Nellie Jack John's children, if he had some fairly soon, could cover the long gap in his history.

'It only needs adjustment,' said David, setting the facts out on a greasy piece of paper. They had arrived breathless in his shed with a mound of chips, some hot, some almost refrozen on the way from the shop. They stamped their feet round the gas-fire. The calculations slithered about between oily marks. 'If he had a boy when he was seventeen . . .'

'Twins,' said Keith. 'Two cocker spaniels. You remember how it is.'

'I can't remember it,' said David. 'It hasn't happened yet.' But he did remember it from years ago at school, and put it from him. He could not bear to read the letters himself, so Keith was doing that for him, gradually telling him what they said.

'Seventeen,' said Keith. He knew he had hurt David, but that David knew he was to feel pain.

'Seventeen,' said David. 'And then he dies, so they don't remember his biological age was seventeen. And in the books they get the age wrong and put seventy-one, not seventeen.'

'No, actually he goes back where he came from,' said Keith, 'and . . .'

'Yes,' said David, seeing what was coming. 'That leaves about a hundred and fifty years from our time back to his.'

'Where he now is if he is seventeen,' said Keith.

'Keep tight hold,' said David. 'This is a paradox, of things that must be the same but have to be different. Anyway, this is only what his grandchildren think in a hundred and fifty years' time. If they think he was seventy-one, and that his father was seventy-one and that his father was seventy-one, then they've got back to his time.'

'And so has he,' said Keith. 'We decided that. He had the twins here, and then went back and married Kath and had their great grandfather.'

'It's either all true,' said David. 'Or none of it's true. But it has to be both, or you can't account for everybody.'

'There isn't anybody,' said Keith. He did not want the idea to come too far alive for David. 'It isn't what we think, but what they think.'

'Grandchildren,' said David. 'We'd best get back.'

The calculations were screwed up into a ball, carried with them and dropped in the bin at the market place.

'Frank thinks Nellie Jack John is up to something,' said David. 'He thinks he's planning to live out in the fields.'

'Wild,' said Keith.

'He hasn't been getting his work done,' said David.

'It's what we sussed out,' said Keith. 'He's in love.'

'There's no one out there,' said David.

'Watch it again,' said Keith, because David was in the road again by the frozen pipe, and a little blue car with painted flames on its sides was thinking of running him down. There was smoke, but not from the painted fires.

'It's Billy,' said Keith.

David did not know what he meant. At the Bowlorama he had not collected or returned shoes himself, and not come forward when the fight had almost started, so he had not read the girl's name. In any case, why should he remember? 'I thought you didn't like them,' he said. 'Kids.'

'It's a girl's name,' Keith explained, and went on to remind David how Nellie Jack John had stared at the shoe-counter girl and been reminded of his Kath.

'Well there,' said David. 'We just decided it was about time he got wed to her and settled down.'

Frank Watson's Land-Rover was at the bottom of the market place, being loaded with sheep-wire and single-strand galvanised wire. The blue car was stopped on a double-yellow line by the sweet shop again.

Once more the mother, in her salt-and-pepper doggy-fur coat was helping the child, this time crossing towards the shop. She bent down and spoke. The child looked at Keith.

'Just go by,' said Keith.

'Yes,' said David, meaning that that was what they were doing in any case. 'Is that actually your grandchild?'

Keith was caught again. Both boys had to stop for a moment to let the child cross the pavement, because she had so much difficulty walking at all.

She changed her direction and took a small step up the hill, reached out one hand, and laid it on Keith's sleeve. She spoke. Her mouth opened like a little pore and closed again, making hardly more sound than a goldfish. She had one crooked front tooth. Her eyes, behind the large glasses, looked into Keith's.

Keith handed her back to her mother, edged round them both,

and went on down the market place. David stood a moment to see that the child did not fall over, then followed Keith.

'But, that isn't called Billy,' he said. 'More like a girl. It must know you from school.'

'No,' said Keith. 'I'd notice. I got to know most of their names. I usually got them on the wrong faces, but I knew the faces. Well, I did yesterday.'

'What did she say to you?' David asked. 'Daddy? Grandpa? Admit to this secret life.'

'I didn't hear,' said Keith.

But he had heard. The little girl had said a name. She had got the name wrong, and because she had spoken quietly and shyly she had not said it very clearly.

But clearly enough she had said, 'Davy.'

If I were David I would understand it, Keith thought. But I can't tell him or ask him. There is something I do not understand.

'It'll come back to you,' said David.

Frank had been tying string to his load of rolls of wire and was getting into the Land-Rover. However, for the moment he was only moving from the store front to a parking slot and setting the parking disc.

'I'm away to your dad, and pay my Lady Day rent, because it's that day tomorrow,' he said to Keith. 'Keep an eye open for Nellie Jack John. He's gone for torch batteries.'

'Right,' said David.

'Are you sure that kid doesn't know you?' said Keith.

'Me?' said David. 'Positive. Well, I don't know *it*.'

'More people know Tom Fool than Tom Fool knows,' said Keith. 'My dad says.'

'That accounts for it,' said David, allowing Keith to be as Tom Fool as he liked. 'I don't know anyone that size. My sister would have been that big, I expect.'

'You never said,' said Keith. 'Until last week. Sunday. This week.'

'I suddenly don't want to be the only one who remembers,' said David. 'I've seen "infant daughter" enough times to forget it means something and it would be that big. She. Not like the letters.'

The little blue car was now moving away from the sweet shop.

'Must live here,' said Keith, gradually assembling the picture of a mother living in Garebrough and working in Middlesbrough. His father, David's father, Frank Watson, all lived and worked in Garebrough, and that seemed almost the only way to live in the town. But it was not.

'Nellie,' said David. 'Look at the fool, he'll get killed. I mean, she'll kill anyone the way she drives in that car.'

'Nothing like being the expert,' said Keith. 'You've driven along the track to Swang, so you know all that could be known.'

All the same, Nellie Jack John was not being the world's wisest pedestrian. He had stopped in the middle of the road out of the market place, and stood clutching a cardboard box and staring at the car. The car passed him, and he resumed his striding walk.

'By,' he said, at the Land-Rover again, 'she's the spit of our Kath. I reckon she's some kin, our Kath will be a fore-elder, what a clipper.'

This was what he always said about his Kath, left beyond the time-warp and all paradoxes.

'You saw her at the Bowlorama,' Keith said to Nellie Jack John.

'Happen,' said Nellie Jack John, not admitting anything.

David considered for a moment. Neither the mother nor the child meant anything to him at all, so he was still thinking about ironing out generation gaps. 'I don't know how what we worked out would cope with someone born here,' he said. 'You have to belong there already. That's the only way it works.'

'Just a few of coals,' Nellie Jack John was saying. 'And forever of milk, into that lear.'

'What's a lear?' David asked. Otherwise he was not listening.

'On the scar abune Swang,' said Nellie Jack John. 'Like a lile barn. I put a drop in the can, and a pocket of coals. I'll tell Frank and he can stop it off my money if I get any.'

'He thinks you're moving off,' said Keith.

'Never,' said Nellie Jack John. 'That's not the way of it. She never much speaks, and she has that jinky-backed bairn and she has to fend. Folk took me in, that's Frank and Eileen, and I'll help turn and turn about. And not a bad spot to live in, isn't Swang, all said.'

Then Frank was back, his business done, and hearing the last things Nellie Jack John said.

'Nowt to do wi' me,' he said. 'Candle ends as well you've taken up, and if that spot gets burned down it's the owners will play pop. But tell them, who's in it, that the lead miners who lived in it kept their powder there, and it didn't all come out when they left. My grandad told me. In there it's a right little house with fireplaces and a dairy and too much running water. I've seen a light there, but I don't know the folk in it haven't a right to it. It hasn't been used in years, since the quarry got so near.'

The Land-Rover shuddered into life. David got in, Nellie Jack John beside him. The Land-Rover went on shuddering across the cobbles.

Keith rubbed his hands together. They were still slippery with oil from the chips.

He went home, faintly unclean from the little girl, also slightly tainted from being called Davy by her. He had to assume he misheard, because no one would call him that; and he had no right to be given the name.

Yet after all, he thought, opening the back door, it's everybody else who knows Tom Fool. Tom Fool does not know them; and perhaps they are right.

VI

The next afternoon Keith rode up to David's house as Dr Wix was driving out of the yard.

'Frank Watson hasn't let him go yet,' said Dr Wix, cranking down the car window.

'I'll go on to the farm,' said Keith. He had been expecting to do so.

'Your nose is dripping,' said Dr Wix. 'Quite a healthy sign in this weather.' He wound the window up and went up the road.

Keith's nose could feel nothing. There was sunshine about today, but the air was still frozen. He shook his head and the drop on his nose splashed golden with sunshine to the tarmac.

He went past the Health Centre and Dr Wix's house, and turned into the road to Swang.

This was the other edge of town from St Agatha's church, and it stopped in the same way. The other side of the last garden wall there were plain agricultural fields, lying idle and snowy. There was a thin unsteady steam rising from the snow, as it sublimed and evaporated in sunshine. In a few hundred yards the houses and the quarry were out of sight. The only sign of the town was the grey brownness of chimney smoke hanging in still air.

The road dropped downhill now towards the high bridge over Jingle Beck in the narrow and deep place called the Giants' Cradle. The road met a track that came down from the moor as the right half of the arm of a T, and turned sharply to be the left half. A vehicle had been using the moor track, as if it were a farm entrance. Keith knew no houses were up there.

However, there was a flash of light high up on the snows, where a car windscreen moved.

Down where Keith was, the dry road ran alongside Jingle Beck, going gradually down the bank to turn in a hairpin at the bridge, The other side of the bridge it ran back the way it had come, now on the far side of the Cradle, and turned away again sharply at the top, continuing to Marrick and Eskeleth and Arkengarthdale.

If there were no signs to tell a driver what was ahead he could well see only the continuation of the road and go straight on into the Cradle. Still in the water below were remains of early motor-cars that had missed the first corner from one side or the other.

The water in the broad depression thirty feet below was buried, frozen under snow. Here and there along its course dark holes showed that it had run after being buried and brought down the snow roof over broad pools, the last places to freeze.

There was a mound and a scatter of broken stone along one slope of the Cradle, the tail of it reaching to the water. A wagon from the quarry had once slid and spilt its load and ended off the road and below it, facing more or less the way it had come.

Dr Wix had been called to the scene. The driver had broken his arm and kenched his back. The wagon had been dragged away and been left at the mouth of the quarry, 'Not looking at all well,' Dr Wix had said. 'The driver was having kittens and the wagon farrowing scale models.'

The quarry was closed nowadays. In its life it had taken a giant shovelful from the side of the hill – a flat bottom with a cliff at the end. People had complained about its noises of blasting, the dust from crushing the stone to fist-size for the blast furnaces of Middlesbrough, and the dangers of the traffic in town. Environmental meetings complained about its shape.

David had disagreed with them at a debate in school. 'If you don't want iron to be made, stop buying cars,' he said. Since the whole aim of everyone at school was to become old enough to drive a car, his argument was disqualified as unreasonable.

In the end the quarry had been abandoned for business reasons.

A tangle of heather fringed the top of its working face, overhanging and drooping, clotted with snow. The owner of the moor lost a few grouse for the shooting season, but gained a better rent. 'And the world goes on,' said Dr Tate at school.

The world was going on at Swang Farm. Keith bumped his way along the track and parked his bike against the house wall.

There was no one about in the yard. Keith followed his ears to where, across two rising fields, Frank's Land-Rover stood, neat at this distance. Beside it three figures were performing a dance, a slow ballet with arms and legs at strange angles and hardly moving. There was the slightest amount of music possible, just an occasional tap-tap-tap-TAP. Once one of the figures fell over, a second one laughed, and the third one shouted.

The first one had been David, the second Nellie Jack John, and the third Frank himself. They were replacing a fence with sheep-wire, a large netting. The wire had been invisible from the house.

Sheep watched, looking indignant and hard done by, having a silent meeting, preparing for the worst.

The work was done by the time Keith came to the fence. 'That's good,' David was saying, pleased at having tidied something that would be left standing. 'Cows, you just milk them and they're filling up again, so it never ends.'

'Doesn't want to,' said Frank. 'You've to have milk every day. But that fence was just wanting to be fettled and we've done it. There's another thing tomorrow, and another the next.'

'But it's a grand thing, sheep-wire,' said Nellie Jack John. 'Possts and stapples.'

'Are you walking?' said Frank, shouldering an unused post.

David drove the Land-Rover down to the yard. Frank walked there sooner, across the field and through a stile. David had to go round by the gates.

Tonight Frank would not let them take the Land-Rover to the lane-end. 'If he's not coming back . . .' he said in the yard.

'School tomorrow,' said Keith.

' . . . then the Land-Rover should stop down here,' Frank went on. 'But put the bikes in and I'll take you to the lane-end. So get away in the kitchen, Keith, and Eileen has the kettle on and a bit of tea. You're welcome to it, deserve it or not; and David right deserves it. Where's Nellie Jack John. Gone off, has he?'

Eileen had the table set. David was washing again at the sink, sent there by Eileen and given a big bar of red soap.

The kitchen smelt of carbolic soap, stove smoke, onion and bacon pie, hot tea, apple pie with cloves, custard, cheese, and traces of pig-muck.

'This is proper, Mother,' said Frank.

Nellie Jack John came in radiating cold, red with it.

'You've landed back, then?' said Frank. 'Eh?'

'I's here,' said Nellie Jack John. 'Nowt ner worse.'

'If you don't land back some time,' said Frank, 'then don't. If it's like that you can get away home.'

'I's here,' said Nellie Jack John. 'See-est-ta.'

'Now, David, some more pie?' said Eileen. 'Frank can have a fresh one at breakfast. Hush, Frank.'

Half an hour later, in the bright moonlight, David and Keith were the far side of the Giants' Cradle but off the road. It seemed like a good idea to leave the road and take a short cut along a little path through two fields above the quarry and over the moor edge.

But the track grew steeper with the fields, and the snow deeper.

The bikes first skidded on the shiny crust, which had been thinned and hardened when sunshine lifted the surface as steam. Then the wheels began to break through the crust. In the end the spokes were twanging on the edges of the surface, and the wheels spun without touching the ground. Then the pedals clogged in snow.

They had to shoulder the bikes and plod through the drifts. The moor gate at the top could not be opened. The snow beyond was nearly impossible to walk across, The surface would hold the weight of a foot for a moment, then give way and leave the walker out of balance, with a bike on top of him.

The moon went behind a cloud and they could see nothing.

'One thing,' said David, leading the way. 'We can track our way back by feel.'

'We can see the town ahead,' said Keith. 'So we just go on.'

Their bikes were up beside them as high as their ears now, riding empty and light on the surface. But all at once Keith's bike tried to get away, as if some fairy rider had mounted weightless on it. The pedals turned and clouted Keith in the ribs (because the top of the snow was so high). The front wheel dipped. Keith was sure the bell rang. The lights came on because the dynamo was switched to run.

The machine escaped from his hand. It was one thing to let the bike fall – it would go nowhere in the snow and come to no harm. But this time the bike was getting away.

David was shouting at the same time. Keith plunged forward to grab the frame. But David, who was in front, turned and pushed Keith away from the bike.

'Give up,' said Keith.

'Keep still,' said David, seriously. Keith kept still. His bike was now on its side and still moving. It was locked where it lay, one pedal in the snow, and turning on that pedal. It was no longer successfully getting away.

Then its front end appeared to be sinking into the snow. The back wheel lifted. Its lights were out now.

Something cracked close to the ground. Keith felt the breaking through the snow and through the ground part of a second later. Following it, and belonging to it, connected by a thread of other sounds, there was a heavy echoing thud, somewhere down below them,

'Hold my arm,' said David. 'Stay there and hold it.'

Keith held it. He still did not know why. David gripped his arm very hard. Keith gripped back.

'Tight,' said David. When the holds were tight enough he reached forward into the dark to the blind bike, took its slowly moving back wheel, and pulled it towards him.

Moonlight suddenly washed the ground again like a new day. Ahead, however, there was no ground. There was only the empty shovel of quarry. They were on the edge of the working face. Behind it, and bringing them to the edge, were the lights of Garebrough.

'We were off the track,' said David. 'We can get to it now.'

'Riding off the edge,' said Keith. 'They could make a film, us against the moon.'

David pulled the rescued bicycle to complete safety. Another overhang of snow broke away and crashed to the floor of the quarry.

'I'll go and look,' said Keith.

'Just come away carefully,' said David. 'Don't stand up. We might be on an overhang already.'

They took some time getting clear, and then some more deciding whether to retrace their footprints entirely or go forward still.

They went forward still, being aware now of the edge of the quarry.

'There's a road somewhere,' said Keith. 'But it hasn't any edges, so we can't tell where it is under the snow.'

They found out very soon. Roads are used. This one was used by a car coming down it, one headlamp dark, the other bright. It came sliding and snarling, the engine roaring when the wheels slipped on the surface on an uphill part.

'If it *is* the road,' said David. 'Not just ploughing about, getting over the cliff.'

But the car knew where it was going, making its way down the hill slowly, if not carefully, its single lamp roving through the sky and over the snow. It came past, and on and out of sight towards the town. It left a hanging sour smell of bad engine that led them to the road.

There they saw that something had often been past, and that the road had been dug into a trench to allow it. There were narrow tyre tracks, and a narrow way between walls.

'We'll go down too,' said David. 'We were daft to come this way.'

Daft with David is all right, Keith thought, lifting his back wheel up and spinning the pedals to bring the lamp on and show him the dark places on the side of the trench. They were car paint, he thought, blue, with touches of red and yellow, like flames.

VII

'It's all rather convincing,' said Keith, one evening. 'It just doesn't work.' They were in David's house, driven from his shed by the continuing cold.

'But nothing to worry about,' said David.

Keith was having difficulty converting x and y into curves on the page.

'Ah, graphs,' said Dr Wix. 'You just put in the co-ordinates and there's your blood pressure. And then you relate that to the pulses of the heart, diastolic and systolic.'

'But he doesn't know what his heart is thinking,' said David.

'No one knows that,' said Dr Wix, 'I find. I'll be next door at evening surgery. If you find a remedy for algebra, don't tell me – I didn't know I wasn't well until you told me how ill I felt.' Then he was off into the frost and across the yard.

'The book has got its x's in a twist,' said Keith. 'Why is the first example $y = x^2 - 4$? There should be an x on its own.' He was shaking his head and pounding it with his fists.

'Yeah, well,' said David unhelpfully. 'It's Gromboolean algebra. Special.'

'I say,' said Keith, after quite a long time. 'It's just come to me. And I'd just proved that the algebra was wrong, the earth is flat, and the sun goes round it; but it was the result of not understanding.'

'It was only wrong between your big ears,' said David. 'So roll up the earth and set the universe going again.'

Keith did that, drew a couple of parabolas to encourage it, and closed the books.

Then they both looked at the fire, Keith not wanting to go out into the frozen streets, David wondering his own thoughts and rummaging in a drawer.

'Before you go,' he said, because Keith was putting books together to carry home.

David had another letter for him. 'I just read the envelopes,' he said. 'And keep them in order. One day I might be able to read them in real time, but now I get turned into being what I was then, and homesickness is an illness I had, and I get changed back to that age and that illness. So I need some things read by you. This is the next one from him.'

'You don't know what it says?' Keith asked. 'Or do you?'

'Don't quite tell me,' said David. 'It's like parabolas. They come on to the page, into the graph, and then back out of sight, and . . . and it bursts inside me.'

And the person on the parabola isn't there any more, Keith thought. David is like poor old x, still existing but off the graph. I wish someone else had to read the letters. Sister Mackenzie? he wondered; and decided that would not be possible.

Dear Davy, the letter read. It was dated in the June of about seven years before. *Scribbling this between patients. It is the Do-It-Yourself day, because the first one, Mr Plumb the plumber, has a hammer toe, and the second one, Mr Chip the carpenter, has an ingrown nail. I don't think the cases are anything to do with each other, but if Mr Sparks the electrician comes in with a short circuit, and Mr Dusty the miller with painful corn, then I shall think there is an epidemic.*

Mummy and I have worked out the date when you should have your new brother or sister or aunt or whatever relation it is. I don't suppose it will make much difference to the family larder – oops, I don't mean we

are going to eat whatever it is — but the day of delivery is the 12th of
August. You will know already that it is called the Glorious Twelfth,
and in honour of it I have been invited as usual to join Mr Solicitor
Heseltine —

'My father,' said Keith, knowing perfectly well what the Glorious
Twelfth was and that his father had always organised what
happened.

'What?' said David. 'Did he write to me? How very mysterious
and unknown and x double-squared.'

'Just mentioned, said Keith, reading on.

— on his grouse moor, kill some dinners full of poisonous but delicious
lumps of lead, have a cold picnic at the Shooting Box while Lord Zig-
Zag's gamekeeper counts the dead birds, and come home smelling of
gunpowder and burnt feathers, and pay money to a charity (probably the
RSPCA) for the fun.

This year I shall be busy with something else, of course. In any case
I am waiting for a rich grouse to pay money to some other charity so that
they can shoot at us on Glorious Friday the Thirteenth, which would fill
Mr Solicitor Heseltine with lead shot — not me because I would have run
away but he would honourably have flown over the guns, being a very
proper gentleman.

Mummy has written to you today, like a proper lady. I have put the
long tape-measure round her twice today (I mean once at a time, this
morning and this afternoon) and find she is growing at a steady pace and
is tending to block out the light, especially after meals.

Love, Dad.

P.S. We hope the tail is still dangling well. If it falls off again we will
try more plastic and elastic surgery.

David held out the envelope. Keith put the letter back in it.

'What was your father doing in there?' said David.

'Nothing legal,' said Keith. 'Just your dad being like he was tonight, just a joke. Insults really, I think, but not real ones.'

'Why ever not?' said David. 'I've never said anything to you that wasn't an insult, have I? Ugly idiot is about right.'

'I hope so,' said Keith. 'Ham-fisted buckets of worms aren't in it. For you that's praise.'

'Pow,' said David, hitting about six inches away from Keith's head.

'Splat,' said Keith, fighting back in the same way and knocking over a table-lamp.

Then they found some of Sister Mackenzie's cake in the kitchen and tidied it away. Keith went home with x and x^2 tucked away in his mind.

'Yes, I remember that year,' said his father, later on. 'Ricky Wix did come out on the Twelfth, but between you and me he could hit nothing and couldn't tackle his food, and was very unhappy. Of course he was. You and David were here all day.'

'David never said a word,' said Mrs Heseltine. 'Has he been talking about it now?'

'Nearly,' said Keith.

'After they were so careful about telling him he would have a brother or a sister, and then, well—'

'By the way,' said his father, 'those shoes of yours that you wore on Sunday – get them out of the house and shoot them. Everything in its place, and the farmyard is the place for them.'

'And,' said his mother, 'I took, and I mean took with a pair of tongs, and washed and I mean twice, that shooting coat that was your dad's which you hung out in the back; and I actually emptied the pockets first and replaced the contents just as they were afterwards. The coat's in your cupboard.'

Keith remembered the boggart's splash of pig-muck on the coat, stinking before it froze, and probably worse when it unfroze. 'I thought the pockets were empty,' he said.

'You always think that,' said his mother. 'But in its time it's been marmalade, and it's been worms, so it could have been worse.'

'I hated marmalade,' said Keith. 'I liked worms.'

The list wasn't over. 'Your trouser pocket's full of sweets,' said his mother. 'A huge sticky mess.'

'I couldn't eat them,' he explained. 'You don't know where they've been.'

'The trousers?' said his mother. 'The usual bottom.'

'Talking of shooting,' said his father, who had not been thinking about clothes and pockets, 'we'll take a walk tomorrow and look at this break-in Constable John Hunter was telling me about. I'd been waiting for the weather to fair up, but it hasn't, so we'll go up in the afternoon.'

'David could come too,' said Keith.

'No problem,' said Mr Heseltine. 'Do you want to stretch your legs too, Dolly?'

'I'll be working all out to get you a big tea for afterwards,' said Mrs Heseltine.

Keith, though, was wondering about David and shooting and the Glorious Twelfth and letters he could still not look at. 'I think shooting, and so on, is one of the things David isn't quite talking about,' he said. 'And if I do, he might think I was meddling.'

'He does keep things in his mind,' said Mrs Heseltine.

'I won't mention it,' said Keith.

'He's other things to work out just now,' said Mrs Heseltine. 'And Keith, time for bed, perhaps?' Of course that meant it was so.

From his window Keith saw again the low translucence of moonlight on snow, and the honey lights of town houses and scattered farms below the moors. On one slope he thought he distinguished the tangled trail of himself and David struggling on bicycles.

But he knew it was not so, that their trail was too small and insignificant to be seen from here. The ruffled mark he saw was the ordinary geography or geology of the landscape, possibly even a belt of trees. One small glow high up above that was there again, faint as a little star, but certainly below the hill.

Don't point, just in case, he remembered. Nellie Jack John said that in his day pointing to the stars would cause you to be struck dead.

VIII

Keith was most used to seeing his father in the house at home, or at chapel. He did not seem like a man for snowy landscape.

He wore a cap with fur round it. Keith wore one like it. It was like wearing a different head – with no attaché case to carry either of them in.

Also it was colder walking about with his father than going about with David. Keith felt his clothes were heavier and held less heat.

'Usually,' he said, 'Mum says keep warm and I automatically do. Now we've put our gear on purposely it doesn't work so well.'

'It's working for me,' said his father. 'Now, we've got to be there in time to look round in daylight.'

Keith was thinking that time would not matter if he and David had been alone on this expedition.

They crossed the river and walked along its bank. Keith had been here with David once, looking for lost pigs. Then there had been some sort of trail to follow. Now there was for a time a trodden path of trampled and refrozen snow, then an untrodden path coming to an end against a solid wall. There was river to one side and a barbed-wire fence the other.

'We'll just lift the fence post away from the wall,' said Mr Heseltine. 'And we're on our way.'

Beyond the fence no one had walked, but in the walls above, the slots of stiles showed one after the other.

'All right for time,' said his father. 'Constable Hunter is to meet us at the Shooting Box at half past three.'

In the top wall of the last field there was a gate, dividing snow from snow. Keith kicked a way in the snow for it to open. There was heather under the snow now.

This was the moor, high on the shoulder of the hill. In a while the curve of the ground hid the gate. Ahead there was another swell of hillside, with here and there a stark face of rock looking out. The crest beyond grew lumps. They were the butts where the guns stood and waited for the birds to fly over during the shooting season.

The Shooting Box was small, and seemed set in the middle of a sea of ice and snow. Beyond it the moor went on for ever, a vaster space than Keith had remembered, a greater upland than there could be space for. He was hardly able to imagine it: though he was seeing it he was unable to fit it into what he knew or could know.

'Back of beyond,' said his father. 'You wouldn't think anyone would expect it was worth breaking into. They wouldn't find anything.'

There was one small construction in front of them, with eternal snow before and behind them. Keith had a strong sensation that they had come out from the known world and were in another. Somewhere between the river and this moment they had crossed a boundary.

At the Shooting Box there were signs that someone had been about: cinders scattered on the snow; clinkery ash with car-tyre marks in them; places where a car had slid about, and wheels been spinning.

'They've been here a time or two,' said Mr Heseltine. 'I think I won't go in until John Hunter is here.'

The track was a flatter stretch in the heather. Whatever car had been here had dug it with its tyres. It vanished some way along the slope, among the irregularities of the moor.

Among those irregularities another shape was moving, a roof, an aerial, a sign, and in a little while the county badge on the side, the check strap like a coachline, and the word 'Police'.

Constable Hunter nodded when he got to the flat place beside the Shooting Box, turned the car neatly about, let his engine run for a moment, and switched off.

He got out and looked at the ground, scraping at cinders with his heel.

'You didn't put these down, sir?' he said. 'If you didn't, someone *has* been here.'

'Someone has been here, John,' said Mr Heseltine. 'What they've wanted I can't imagine.'

'Some folk are daft as brushes,' said the policeman. He went away round the building and came back in a moment.

'They took the shutters off the windows and put 'em down tidily,' he said. 'And the windows are still complete. If you've got the key we'll go through the door.'

He put the key in the lock and turned it three times. The lock fell off and clattered on a stone flag inside.

Mr Heseltine bent to pick it up.

'Don't touch,' said the policeman. 'We might need fingerprints. It'll be town lads up here to drink beer. The place will be full of cans, and they'll be evidence too. Mess and that.'

He was looking through the doorway into a passage beyond. There were two more doors in one of its walls, leading to the rooms. The other wall was covered with hooks. Keith could remember a photograph at home of a wall covered in hooks, and the hooks draped with dead grouse.

'Nothing to see here,' said the policeman. 'I can smell there's been a fire in a fireplace. And it isn't so cold as it might be,

61

considering. I'll take a look in.' He moved in. 'Best wait,' he said. 'It's funny stuff, evidence. Do you remember the lad who wrote his name in the visitors' book at that factory in Gallowfields?'

'Told me,' said Mr Heseltine, 'that reading and writing were both dangerous and he wished he hadn't been taught 'em. Thought he was obeying the law enough by writing his name during the house-breaking job.'

'There isn't a visitors' book here, but there's been a visitor,' said the policeman. 'I won't say it's tidy, but it hasn't been messed about. This looks like housekeeping, and be travellers, or the like.'

The first room had a long, broad, stone shelf running from inside the door to the window. On it stood a green plastic washing-up bowl. The bowl had water in it, and in the water two or three plates and cups, and some spoons and knives.

In a wooden box below the shelf there was a packet of breakfast cereal. In a jug on the shelf was some milk.

'Fresh yet,' said Constable Hunter, bending to sniff it. 'And that water in the bowl should by rights have been frozen this last month and more.'

At the far end of the shelf, by the window, was a cardboard shoe-box, its lid standing up at one end like a tall bed-head.

'Well,' said Constable Hunter, 'I shouldn't be too worried. They broke the lock, I know, but I don't think it's worth following up. I can sort this out. Just check in the other room first.'

Keith wondered what the shoe-box held to turn Constable Hunter's opinion that way. But he was not expected to be interested in it. Constable Hunter casually closed him out of the room.

The other room had the fireplace. The fire had been burning coal. There was a heap beside it.

'There's been coal here many a year,' said Mr Heseltine. 'We've had many a grand blaze in it, at the last shoot before Christmas.'

'These coals are wet,' said Constable Hunter. 'If they'd been long here they'd be dry. If the fire had been long out they'd be frozen. So whoever it is isn't long gone. And the throat of this fire is still warm. And you can smell the smoke nearly fresh. Wood smoke, though, not coal.'

There was a lantern on a table by the window. There was a drawing book beside it, with some school-like drawings in it. There was no name on it.

'Children,' said Constable Hunter. 'A word at school will stop it. They don't want to be here in this weather, or any, come to that.'

'Children,' said Mr Heseltine. 'It wasn't children had a car out there, and not just once but many a time.'

Keith was looking about and wishing there was a fire and large convivial food and hunters sure of themselves. He lifted a sheet of cardboard that was propped against the wall and looked behind it.

There was nothing on the wall. But on the back of the cardboard there were three photographs, of a woman, a woman and a little boy, and of a woman and a man.

The man was Dr Wix, much younger. Keith did not know the woman, or the little boy. He thought he should not know anything about these pictures, or why they were here, or what they were doing. Because in spite of not knowing the child or the woman he was certain who they were. With a sort of sorrow he knew why they were there and why he did not know they had been.

He dropped the cardboard back into place, and went out of the Shooting Box. His mind was racing about and not managing to think. It only told him to get out of sight of the two men, now no longer friendly Constable Hunter or his own father, but people who ought not to know about pictures of Dr Wix in this far-out place.

David, he thought, was excluding him from his thoughts; David was showing him letters to keep him away, not to allow him closer;

63

David was becoming more private, not more public. Keith felt himself not to be the friend he thought he was, that he was being fobbed off with trifles to keep him happy.

He kept moving because the cold day was becoming a colder evening. He walked away from the door, round the police car, looking at tyre marks, wondering what vehicle caused them. Then, to feel he was doing something useful and not merely pursuing his own thoughts, he followed Constable Hunter's footprints round the little house.

The constable's track was not the only one. Someone had come up the hill to the corner of the building several times, or several people once.

Someone had visited the edge of the rock the building stood on. Here one person had made many tracks, because the purpose had been to empty slops of different sorts – tea-bags and apple cores, a label from a soup tin – down a cleft, where they had all frozen.

Unexpectedly, he was on the edge of the hill. He understood at once why he had felt the Shooting Box was completely in the middle of a great unbroken plain. Because they had been walking on high ground, and the air was not totally clear, he had seen straight past the Shooting Box, right across a dale beyond, and to farther hills at the same level.

Now he saw the land dropping away below, and he knew where he was. He had been there many times. Straight ahead, diminutive, with a toy light glowing at a window, was Swang Farm. In its yard Frank was turning a model tractor.

To the left the moor sloped down towards Jingle Beck. The Giants' Cradle and the bridge were below and out of sight. Even more to the left the town lights were coming on, and the castle was black against mottled snow.

Keith heard a sneeze. He turned to look the other way, along the hillside. The sneezer sniffed, spoke to himself, so that Keith knew it was not a woman, and came into sight, plodding along at a good pace, rubbing his nose with his sleeve.

Nellie Jack John was carrying a milk can and a small bag. He reached the wall of the Shooting Box, was beyond it for a moment, and then turned down the hill again. He was not now carrying milk can or bag.

'We'll take a ride down, Keith,' said his father, coming round from the other side. 'We've had our walk.'

'Nothing to detain us now,' said Constable Hunter.

If only I understood as easily as that, thought Keith.

IX

Mr Heseltine jammed the door lock back into place and then gave up on the cold metal. There was no way of mending it now, and no point in doing so until the intruders had been found and warned off.

'Washing-up,' said Mr Heseltine. 'And that shoe-box.'

Keith had not seen inside the shoe-box. Without its contents it had no significance at all, and not much more if the contents were shoes. He sensed that he would not be told anything. He had a feeling too that he ought not to know or want to know, because of being excluded by David.

'I'll have a word at the schools,' said Constable Hunter, 'Big children can get into worse trouble than little ones.'

Not specifically talking about David, Keith decided.

Now that three people were in his car, all the windows steamed up at once. The policeman opened his window to let the damp breath out and turned the fan on loud. From Keith's place in the back seat all he got was extra noise and no heat.

'What animal was that?' Constable Hunter wondered at the point where Keith's and David's walking and cycling tracks met the road. There was a messy mark across the snow.

'The barghest,' said Mr Heseltine. 'Ghost dog, big as a calf. Walks at night.'

Keith said nothing because he might be blamed. Mr Heseltine's mention of the barghest was a fanciful joke, but he would not like the fancy destroyed at once. Keith did not want to confess that he

67

and David had nearly gone over the edge of the quarry at night, like a barghest. He remembered thinking he had seen these tracks from his window at night, yet in broad daylight now and close to them he could hardly make them out.

'The same kids,' said Constable Hunter. 'Not you, eh Keith?'

It was difficult to answer the question, now that the track and the Shooting Box were mingled in it. Dr Tate at school had pointed out that the mixing of things into one question was a sort of logical lie and there was no single answer.

'If you mean, have I been to the Shooting Box,' he said, 'the answer is no. If you mean, did I make the track in the snow, the answer is yes. However, I am not a barghest.'

Constable Hunter turned down the fan, so that what followed was almost silence.

'It was a messy question,' said Constable Hunter.

'And I'm put in my place,' said Mr Heseltine. 'We believe this witness.'

'Witness?' said Constable Hunter. 'More like the lawyer in the case. Keith, you are following in your father's footsteps and already have a legal mind.'

But however much Keith thought about what he had seen in the Shooting Box, he came to no conclusion.

Coming past the corner by the Monks' Infirmary, Constable Hunter beeped his horn at a small blue car with painted flames along its side, which was moving out into the road in an uncertain manner.

'No point going in there,' he said. 'It's been closed this last eighteen months. The young lady will have been a nurse, maybe. But I think she'll be in a traffic incident before long. If I get the chance I'll have a word with her.'

He chauffeured them to the house and went on his way. Looking for ears to have words in, Keith thought. His father went round to the back of the house.

'I don't want to interfere,' Mr Heseltine said. 'We don't want to interfere. It wouldn't come right from me, and Hunter didn't see it and you and I did. I saw it upset you.'

Keith knew what he was talking about. It was another logical problem, but not so simple as the instance Dr Tate had given. However, since David . . .

'You know what I mean,' said Mr Heseltine. 'You looked and you walked out, and I looked, but Hunter didn't. That was Ricky Wix, and Liz, and David when he was small. He's long lived in yesterday, and never got over his mother. So just now things will be difficult for him and he'll not know how to put things together. What do you say nowadays? He wants a bit of space. If that space is the Shooting Box then he's welcome to it, tell him. Just, it would have been better if he'd said. He didn't need to ask, but he wouldn't know that. If he wants to spend some time there he's welcome.'

'I don't think I can tell him,' said Keith.

'Maybe not,' said Mr Heseltine. 'But you might have told us and saved Constable Hunter an afternoon when he might have been at home.'

Keith was not able to say anything, either to his father or to David. This time the logical lie had not been a question, so there was no need to reply. But in fact if he had known that David was using the Shooting Box he would still have said nothing, because he did not know it was the Shooting Box. It was that from his father's point of view, but from Nellie Jack John's it was a lear on the hill, and from Frank Watson's it was one of the lead mine buildings called the Powderhouse.

There was just one link, that Constable Hunter had referred to explosives once, and Frank had also said that gunpowder had been stored there. But there was no way of relating two small pieces of information until you knew they were the same.

So he would not have said anything, and could not have. 'I didn't know, already,' he said.

'That is an Americanism of little meaning,' said his father. 'Just tell him he's welcome.'

'And have a nice day,' said Keith. 'If we're doing American.'

'I don't know about solicitor,' said Mr Heseltine. 'You'll end up in the dock or as the judge. So take care.' He was pleased, and took Keith's arm. 'We'll go in and get our teas,' he said, opening the door. 'Mother, watch out for this lad; he's giving as good as he gets and we'll have to watch our step.'

But Keith, one way and another, in spite of tracing the logical lies, could not tell what was happening, or why; or even to whom.

He put forward a guess to himself, that the shoe-box still held shoes, and that they had belonged to David's mother. That would make a sort of sad sense. Any sense was better than none.

But something else remained. Who had been going there in a car? A blue car, with flame paint that has rubbed off on a hardened snowdrift?

X

Late that night there was a small star below the rim of the hill overlooking the town. Keith could not convince himself that it was, or that it wasn't, one of the windows of the Shooting Box. That was because he did not know where he was looking and, in spite of seeing that scene night and morning, had not noted detail that had no significance.

By daylight, in the morning, the very shape of the hills was changed by the town below it. The general effect was of snow-covered moors, Keith thought, and that was what you would call it. In fact there was so much to break the whiteness that a dirty speckle was more accurate. Any small building was lost in that dirty speckle, indistinguishable from the patchy background.

Keith was also unsure about what he could say to David now. It did not seem right to transmit messages from his own household. It did not seem right not to. It seemed right to help David in any possible way; it seemed right too to leave him to work matters out for himself. The conflict of possibilities left him without anything to say.

I am just an ugly idiot, Keith thought. I am without the sort of sadness that shows by working through the burdens of life with a cheerful countenance and a sense of humour and enquiry. Idiots are merely cheerful and are otherwise without thoughts.

Dr Tate said the same, fairly often. 'An idiot has no external reference,' he had said. 'A fool has no internal reference. One can't

71

help it; the other can.' Keith felt he couldn't help it, and began to understand the words.

But of course, David was neither fool nor idiot, but a wounded person. Since there was some History to sort out one evening that week, Keith went up.

They were in the house, getting books open, which sometimes cannot be done immediately.

'You have to be ready for the words,' said David. 'Before they grab you and drown you in The Causes of the American Revolution and Changes in Political Emphasis during the course of the War.'

'I'm not ready for it,' said Keith. 'We've got our history man.' Nellie Jack John was their history man, born before the American Revolution and knowing nothing about it, only that 'Some folk had gitten across there and were keeping pigs and that, nowt ner worse, nowt ner better.'

'Take your coat off,' said David. 'We have to think of something.'

'We want one of your dad's funny stories,' said Keith. He was wondering whether he had any right, or duty, to talk about David's family. The words died away as he said them.

'I'll look again one day,' said David. 'They're there. I shan't lose them.'

Keith pulled a sleeve inside out as the shooting coat came off. 'It shrinks when she washes it,' he said, because it was that particular coat. He flung it on the bed.

'The slaves wanted to be free,' said David. 'But that didn't work, did it? Did that stop being a cause during the war?'

Keith was shaking the coat into submission, finding it lumpy. It had draw-strings to pull the hood tight and the hem in. It also had a curious loose end hanging out at one side. Keith pulled it out from the pocket where it was.

It came free of something as he pulled. He had no idea what it was. It was firm but floppy. It was grey, possibly made of rubber.

Definitely made of rubber, he decided, and looked at it more closely. It was seven inches long and triangular in section, at one end about a quarter of an inch across, and tapering to a point at the other. He still had no idea what it was, until it came to him that it was the tail of a mouse.

'Not a real one,' he said, putting it on the table.

David glanced at it, looked back to the book, and then looked at the thing once more. 'It,' he said, and that was his sentence and comment. He half rose from his chair, with his fingers supporting him on the table.

Keith, expecting some wild joke from David, was now finding the lumpy thing in the pocket of the coat, without understanding why anything was there at all.

'I thought so,' he said, pulling out the grey-brown of a toy of some sort, from tailless rump down to pointed nose, whiskers worn away with time and handling.

He put it on the table and rolled it over. 'Home-made,' he said. 'Not a shop one,' because it plainly was not. There was a hard centre to the creature, and a keyhole in the side.

A label on the threadbare and once-pink belly had a capital letter D stitched on it.

None of this had any significance for Keith. He assumed his mother had put it in his pocket. But she did not play meaningless jokes. She had said, too, that she had replaced everything in the pocket of the coat, but he had put nothing there, and knew nothing about it. It had nothing to do with his work experience at school, because he had not worn the coat there.

'It's a mystery,' he was beginning to say, looking for the wastepaper-basket, ready to throw it away and go back to ancient transatlantic quarrels.

For some reason the table was shaking. David was standing up and quivering with some emotion. Keith had not seen his face so filled with some expression of hatred. He thought at first the mouse was being hated.

When David hit him with his right fist he knew he was hated. When the left fist came across the table and hit him too, he knew something was truly wrong.

Then the table was turned over, and David leapt on him, hitting and kneeing, and shouting.

What he shouted Keith did not understand.

'That's Muz,' David shrieked. 'That's Muz. You stole Muz, you bloody thief, you stole him, you stole him, you shouldn't have been there, and it's all your fault.'

Keith was hurt. His nose was bleeding. There was a gushing scratch by his right ear. He was in agony from David's knee up between his legs. David had meant to hurt.

Keith had had fights before. But not this one. This fight was meant to kill, he was sure. He did not know how to continue it, and he could not see. All his attention was now on the toy mouse.

'Muz,' David was saying still, 'Muz, Muz,' and tears were not being wept but running continual.

David turned from Keith, collapsed on the bed, and curled himself round Muz, and sobbed and sobbed.

Then Dr Wix was in the room. 'Now come on,' he was saying. 'You can have your romps somewhere else. I heard from across the yard, David.'

David was beyond noticing him.

'David,' said Dr Wix, looking at Keith, deciding that he was not to blame so there was no further cause for scolding. 'David.'

David lay where he was, curled up tight, and sobbed.

'He attacked me,' said Keith. 'It's that toy.' The rubber tail was on the floor. He picked it up and held it out to Dr Wix.

Dr Wix looked at it and knew what it was. He sat on the bed, with one hand on David's shoulders, and looked at Keith enquiringly.

'I do not know,' said Keith. 'It was in my pocket. I do not know what it is.'

'Muz,' said Dr Wix. 'Davy.'

David spared a hand for his father's hand.

'Keif,' he said, like a baby. 'I'm sorry. I didn't mean it. You didn't know. There must be some other reason, how you got him. The key is in the drawer of my desk.'

Keith picked up the table first. He did not feel he had to leave. David was now sitting up a little, and leaning against his father, but looking at his friend.

That is what friends are sometimes for, Keith thought, picking up books. David snivelled and had to be lent a handkerchief. He had a row of sobs, and then held his breath against them.

Keith turned to the desk drawer. His knees were jerking. His hands were hardly working.

Inside the drawer was the bundle of letters, and packets of chocolate.

'At the back,' said David. 'On a little box. Muz's box. Muz's hole.'

The box had careful printing on it in large rounded letters – long ago, or it might have been during this very term at a primary school by its child. 'MUZZLE' they said. Mousehole, Keith read, with throbbing sight and blurred vision, reluctant eyes.

Keith brought out the key. David's trembling hand wound Muz desperately. Muz had tiny wheels in his chest. Thorax, Keith decided. David sat up to put him on the table and watch. Muz moved about the table without falling over the edges, each time turning away. Then he twirled and stopped, his party trick over.

'Tail still loose, I see,' said Dr Wix. 'We never did manage to make a job of that.'

'I think I'll go to bed,' said David, curling up again. 'Read to me, Daddy.'

'Can you give me a moment?' said Dr Wix. 'I've got the man in the surgery who spits out sixpenny pieces whenever he thinks of Australia. I'll just have a word with Sister and she can sort him out.'

'I'll see you,' said David to Keith. 'You'd better get something from her too.'

When Keith left, David was crouched on his bed, a wet thumb now and then in his mouth, holding Muz, considering how to fit the tail on. That was the tail in the letters, Keith concluded. The man who spat sixpenny pieces when he thought of Australia was yet to come. He went down the stairs with Dr Wix, his feet awkward, his elbows shaky, his belly hollow.

'The problem is to get him not to think of Peru,' said Dr Wix, referring to the patient again, pressing telephone buttons, ringing across to the Health Centre, watching Keith and having a hand ready in case it was needed. 'Then he spits out badly inflated South American money,' he continued when he had spoken words Keith did not listen to. 'Go across to Sister, and she'll sort you out.'

'Spitting sixpenny pieces?' said Sister Mackenzie. 'No. The last patient has gone, and it wasn't that sort of complaint at all. Dr Wix says I'm to take you home when I've treated you. A quarrel, was it?'

'Accident,' said Keith. That was to be his story.

'Sit on the couch,' said Sister Mackenzie.

'Toilet,' said Keith, finding his way to it. He stood there in a bright light and then came out again.

'I couldn't do a drop,' he said, slightly anxious about that. But David had not actually got his knee there.

'I said it was a fight,' said Sister Mackenzie. 'But not one you picked. Aye, it happens. I trained in Glasgow, and in casualty there was the same problem even if they were full of the lager. It won't last. You'll be right as rain before long.'

'I'm cold,' said Keith, sitting on the couch.

'Everything will come back,' said Sister Mackenzie. 'It's the body's defences. It's a bit shock the now, and if you're like this, then how's the other fellow?'

Keith could say nothing about the other fellow. He thought the other fellow was in a worse state, but one of a different kind. But there was plainly nothing to be done now.

Sister Mackenzie dabbed him with a twitchy liquid and stuck a plaster under his eye.

'That's you patched,' she said. 'I was just brewing a cup of tea, so perhaps you'd like one before I run you home.'

When she filled the kettle Keith had to hurry to the lavatory. Things were beginning to work again.

But what had happened with David he could not account for; nor for the reason behind it. Of course there had been a tail in Dr Wix's letter to David, but that could not possibly be related to anything from Keith's pocket. Or could it be, in some way?

He could hardly think. Sister Mackenzie drove him to his door and said goodnight. Keith went down beside the house, and then came out again. He was not quite ready to go indoors and needed a walk round the market place.

There were cars parking and a crowd going to the theatre, and he walked among them, to be among people but not have to be anyone or explain anything, but to see normality and belong to it.

One of the parked cars started a noisy engine and drove away. Under the streetlamps it was a dingy monochrome, but shop lights showed the blue paint and the flames. Billy drove it, her hair puffed out in her wild but deliberate style. Beside her was a smaller figure.

High up on the hill there was no solitary light. Later, going to bed, Keith perceived either it or some low star.

XI

'Dr Wix just checking up,' said Mrs Heseltine in the morning, putting down the early telephone while Keith dragged a last cornflake from the waxy corner of the packet.

'How's David?' said Keith.

'David?' said his mother. 'He was checking on you. You and David had a quarrel, or something.'

'No,' said Keith. 'He just beat me up. He was moody. That's all. He must have had a reason.'

'A reason is no excuse,' said his father. 'Are you going to do something about it?'

'I'll ask him why,' said Keith. 'It won't be a mystery but an excuse. There nothing to see a solicitor about, Dad. I'm not taking him to court.'

'I'll assume justice was done,' said his father.

Mrs Heseltine said, 'We make allowances for David, losing his mother and so on so young; and there was all the time he was missing the year before last.'

There was no way of explaining that for David no time at all had elapsed between vanishing into a time-warp and coming out of it again.

'Never mind that,' said Mr Heseltine, 'Just at the moment he won't be knowing what to think. And it's my belief Ricky Wix doesn't know either.'

Mrs Heseltine smiled. 'It's so suitable. We shan't love Ricky or David any less.'

'What are you saying?' said Keith. But his mother was now abstractedly looking in the teapot and deciding the tea-bag had gone past its brew-by date. She threw Keith an out-of-date smile to match, and took the pot to the kitchen.

Mr Heseltine was checking the calendar on the wall. 'Where's my licence? I have to go down to Rodbers.' Rodbers was where he bought fishing tackle and other sports goods. 'Dolly, do you know? Keith?' Keith did not know, and his mother was not hearing.

'She was always soft on Ricky Wix,' said Mr Heseltine. 'Lucky man, I say, to be out of reach or otherwise occupied.' Mrs Heseltine clattered the washing-up.

At school that day Keith was never in the same group as David for lessons or dinner. Their time-warps intersected once only in a corridor.

'You all right?' David asked. 'Apart from ugly.'

'OK,' said Keith. 'But I don't understand.'

'I'm the one that doesn't understand,' said David.

'But what don't you understand?' said Keith.

'Why you had that . . . you know what,' said David. 'You aren't to say its name. That's private. It was all private.'

'We both don't understand,' said Keith.

'In your pocket?' said David. 'You must.'

'No,' said Keith.

'You didn't know what it was,' said David. 'But you have seriously got to know where it came from. I apologise for what I did, but I have to know.'

A bell screamed about the school's time-warp, and they continued to their different destinations.

Even when they were talking about the toy mouse they were looking different ways, seeing different things. There was no way towards understanding.

It's like a disease from Dr Wix's letters, Keith thought, the patient having an affliction that puts things he has never seen in his pocket, for which he is beaten up and not enjoying it like a friend.

Keith waited at the gate after school, but David had gone ahead. Keith saw him later, on the high pavement opposite the Monks' Infirmary.

I have not done anything I know of, Keith thought to himself. I have had it done to me. He patted his pockets to ensure that the disease was in remission and no strange symptoms had arrived.

At home, after tea, Mr Heseltine was opening one of his cupboards outside the room. Keith's mother said, 'I went and had a talk with Dr Wix.'

'Boys will be boys,' said his father.

'There wasn't any need,' said Keith, meaning his mother's visit.

'You were bleeding at breakfast,' said his mother. 'That's need enough. He said David was very sorry and unhappy about what he did.'

Keith's cheek had now dried enough to feel as he ate, a scab to be gently explored with fingers looking forward to peeling it off clean with a satisfying tickle, leaving a piece of dead self on your hand, but the rest of you still whole.

His mother was saying, ' . . . but he was very distressed, Keith, when you brought that toy mouse from your pocket without a word of explanation.'

'I have got zero explanation,' said Keith. 'Nought point nought nought nought recurring.'

' . . . with the tail off it,' said his mother. 'I hope that wasn't my fault.'

Keith looked at her with a sort of horror. How could it be her fault? Or was he hearing things wrong? 'I get it,' he said. 'I'm concussed again. I need an X-ray or a scan. Aspirin, headache.'

His father then came back into the room and said, with a nightmare effect, 'We'll get the guns ready.' He was carrying one.

Guns always look ready for use, smooth and loaded, pointing in some direction.

He's mad too, Keith thought, with an actual painful twitch in the belly, his tea rattling, alarm prickling his elbows. The realities of gang warfare, like a play last year at the theatre, came into his mind. Why do I always have terrible thoughts and never jokes? he wondered.

'It was nothing,' he said, as sensibly as he could through jarring images from the play, of civil war, of actors near the edge of the stage, stampeding among the stalls with knives, large, loud, impersonal; Mercutio, David, truly dead. 'You wouldn't shoot a bicycle just because I fell off it.'

'I believe he *is* concussed,' said Mr Heseltine. 'I am talking about clay-pigeon shooting tomorrow, which I assume you have forgotten, or why this wild talk about bicycles? I went to Rodbers for cartridges this morning, some of them tracer, so you will see how far off target you are, Keith. What are you talking about?'

He heard Keith explain about the mouse and its tail, and how his mother now thought it was her fault. It was his turn to think things were astray.

'I do not understand the logic of this,' he said. 'What you are both saying is not rational. Dolly, what are you talking about?'

'David,' said Mrs Heseltine.

'I'm talking about Mum,' said Keith. 'I'm not hearing her right. I don't understand anything. If I was the bicycle you would shoot me.'

'You do not have to be mad,' said his father, 'Though it might help. This conversation is loaded, and the first thing to do is to take the cartridges out of it.' He broke open the gun to show what he meant. It was empty. 'Until you can't fire it it's just as useful empty as it is when it's full. We do not need to discuss concussion. You are talking about different things without realising it. Or you are talking about the same thing in different ways. Let us sort it out.'

'That's what Dr Tate says,' said Keith. 'Argue about the same thing if you can. If you can't, just make more noise than your opponent.'

'Sounds like life as I see it in court,' said Mr Heseltine. 'We'll start by sorting out what we are talking about. Keith, from the beginning. Tell me what happened yesterday.'

'I got to David's house,' said Keith. 'We were in his room, doing the American Revolution again.'

'Quite right,' said his father. 'It needs work. They got it wrong on the day.' One of his hump-backed jokes, Keith realised. Where I get it from.

'Hush,' said Mrs Heseltine. 'This is serious.'

'It happened after Nellie Jack John got lost in time,' said Keith.

'We're not having any more of the time business,' said his mother, not liking to be reminded that Keith himself had been lost too. To Keith his absence had lasted five minutes or so, but it brought weeks of distress on his parents.

'Not relevant,' said Mr Heseltine, dabbing a wad with oil richer than bicycle oil, wiping the blue barrel of the gun. 'Doesn't relieve the situation. Then what did you talk about or do?' He pulled the wad through the barrels and seemed to think it became cleaner. It had already been bright.

The work would be done again after the shoot, Keith thought, so this cleaning was a ritual, nearly religious.

'When I got it out he jumped on me,' said Keith. 'The thing in that coat pocket. Sort of a toy mouse, but first its tail.'

'Made of rubber,' said his mother. 'About this long.'

'You don't know,' said Keith.

'I do,' said his mother. 'I said it was there.'

'It's no good,' said Keith. 'I'll have to have the brain scan. You didn't tell me anything.'

'I carefully did,' said his mother.'

'Tell us again, Dolly, and it'll soon be cleared up,' said his father. 'Right, Keith, you can clean your mother's gun.' He handed over an ungainly, bent and open heavy thing of wood and blue metal, with two little enclosed legs – the triggers in their guard.

'You got that coat,' said his mother, 'the one your dad handed on, yes? Covered in pig-muck or something, and I made you hang it out in the back. The smell didn't go away so I washed it. It isn't waterproof any more anyway. I took things out of the pockets, and I put them back. I told you.'

'Careful not to pull the triggers when the gun is opened at the breech,' said Mr Heseltine. 'As well as at other times.'

Keith thought about what his mother said with the part of his mind that was busy not pulling triggers. What she said was true in some ways. It dealt with the problem of her madness, but not quite with the problem of his own. 'There was nothing in the pockets,' he said. 'No mouse and no tail.'

'They were both there,' said Mrs Heseltine. 'When the shooting coat was dry I put them back. I just thought it was a school mascot.'

'The primary school?' said Keith, 'It can't be that, because I didn't wear that coat there.'

Mr Heseltine rapped on the table with a cleaning rod. 'The court will come to order,' he said. 'We have solved one part of the problem, but not proved where the evidence came from, or what it is.'

'I know what it is,' said Mrs Heseltine. 'I was going to say at the beginning. Dr Wix explained. It was a toy that Liz made, David's mother. The tail never did stay on very well.'

'It kept falling off and having to be repaired,' said Keith. 'It was surgery, Dr Wix said.'

'So you do know something about it,' said Mr Heseltine. 'Or am I the one with concussion? Put a bit more oil on that wad.'

'David showed me some letters,' said Keith, pulling the wad

through. 'He didn't look at them, but I did. He asked me to. I didn't know what they were about. One letter talked about a tail that kept falling off. I thought it was private, but it must have been the mouse's.'

He thought about Mr Bazangalong for a moment, while he squinted along both barrels. He decided against mentioning him. Mr Bazangalong was particularly private too.

'Yes,' said his father. 'Quite. But what else?'

'Why did David put it into my pocket?' Keith said. 'And when?'

'He didn't,' said Mrs Heseltine. 'He didn't have it. He was upset because he had not seen the mouse since he gave it to his mother when she was in hospital expecting that baby. He was very little. He thought it had looked after him so well away at school that it would look after her. But we know he lost her and the baby too.'

'He would never think about the baby,' said Mr Heseltine. 'Would he?'

'I shouldn't think so,' said Mrs Heseltine. 'He never mentions it, though that isn't quite the same as never mentioning his mother. But I haven't quite said about the mouse. You see, it never came back from the hospital. David was unhappy about that, because his mother had made it and it was one less thing for him to remember her by. So when you pulled it out of your pocket, Keith, David did not know what he was doing. He has an idea, which is natural, that you took it all those years ago and caused the tragedy.'

Keith considered this information. The play with street fighting had been a tragedy. The world's greatest love story, it said on the programme.

'That is a good excuse,' he said. 'I think I would have been worse. I would have been awful.'

His play would have been banned, he decided.

Mr Heseltine took the gun from him, because it was being waved about.

'It was a shock, Dr Wix thinks,' said Mrs Heseltine. 'He didn't know why you did it to him. It was very cruel, he thought.' She took the gun from her husband and rubbed up some fine patterns on its flank.

'If it went to the Infirmary,' said Keith, 'how did it get into my pocket all these years later?'

'As usual we don't know,' said his father, shaking his head. 'But at least we know what we're talking about.'

He locked the guns and the discussion away. 'We'll go round in circles otherwise,' he said, clamping the cupboard doors firmly into their frames.

From the middle of the next day Keith was cold through. The clay-pigeon shoot was up on the edge of the moor, far beyond the Shooting Box, in a patch of snow crusted brittle with grains of ice. A scanty fire of ling burned like a rodent ulcer through the frost of the moor.

Down to one side the high fields of Swang Farm spread up to the moor wall. Swang was beyond and below again, a chimney smoking in the still air. Frank was working in the yard.

On the hill sheets of snow began to be speckled with black fragments of clay pigeon. The sky itself was cracked with sound. Keith had to wait and wait between turns. His father loaded tracer into Keith's mother's gun for Keith to fire. He got three clays out of eight, one of them being hit so slightly it only chipped and flew off-course. It and five others broke on impact with the snow.

His mother was the best shot. 'I don't know how to do it,' she said. 'It just happens.'

'She never manages to shoot an actual bird,' said Mr Heseltine. 'But she's a natural.'

Keith stamped about to keep warm. The men at the meeting warmed themselves with rum. Keith had a can of Coke. Shot went on assaulting the sky.

In the middle of the afternoon someone began shooting in the fields below. It was Frank Watson killing a running rabbit. It somersaulted, kicked, and lay stretched and still. Frank slit a back leg, put the other through it, and hung it at his belt. He came to see the clays being shot.

The shooters began to tease him about his gun. It was a muzzle-loader, they said, and had Frank brought some nails to fill it with?

Keith thought of Muz and his box, Muzzle.

Frank grinned and shot all the clays they could send him. He took two drinks of rum, and went back down to the farm with his rabbit.

Behind him Nellie Jack John picked his way down from the Shooting Box, carrying a milk can.

'He should have come shooting with us,' said Mr Heseltine. 'I don't mean John Cherry, but David Wix. Mind, Cherry is a sensible lad, and lost both his parents, so long since we can't find their graves, so they've something to say to each other. But David will be brooding in the Shooting Box, and it's not the healthiest thing for him. Maybe we should stop him. I don't mean stories about gunpowder being hidden – if those had been true we couldn't have had fires all these years without being blown to pieces. I mean that he should have got over some things, and if he hasn't perhaps someone ought to have a word somewhere else.'

They mean he is mad, Keith thought. It would explain most things, but even if he is brooding at the Shooting Box he is not mad. He is better than normal and they are less than normal. Actual normal does not exist, because that is what I am.

They went down the hill in Land-Rovers, leaving the trapman and his trap to find their own way.

At home Keith and his father cleaned the bitter empty guns again, with strips of grimy cloth, and locked them away.

Later on, sitting in bed, he saw overcast sky reflecting the sodium streetlamps, and watched windows of lit rooms. Tipping his focus to one side to see more clearly, he found one small star on a distant hill. This little light was the tracer of some shot to come, the foreshock of time-warps. Because what else was there? And why was David there at times, with his mother's photograph, turning away from those who knew him? What light from yonder window shone? Keith felt his cheek for reality. The firm scab went to sleep with him.

At the edge of sleep something like a memory from another person, or like an explanation in another language, entered his mind. It was shouldered aside by sleep. In the morning its existence but not its content was waiting to be noticed and ignored.

XII

'It's a bad do, is some of that,' said Nellie Jack John, blowing steam off the top of a mug of tea. He was with Keith and David in the Castle Café in the market place. He was talking about his day at the university in York, where he went once a month to tell them about his life two hundred years ago.

David was quiet. This was the first time he and Keith had met on purpose since he had attacked Keith. Before then they had never considered that their meetings were events. This evening they both were taking notice of their manners and had met on neutral ground.

'I've gitten used to t'road in,' Nellie Jack John went on. 'Folk just think I's a country lad, and I is. But them fellows 'at asks questions, why, I don't know, they ken nowt, and there's yan lile booger allus teks anither part and contraries me. They were wanting to ken about America, but I told them I were niver theer, but there's my uncle Nellie Peter gone to the colony and wrote back and said there was plenty of hag-worms that might kill a man, and this lile fellow laughs and says it's only a tale and I hadn't to get telling yarns. But there's this letter back at Eskeleth to show him, and I could fetch it if I knew the road.'

He was talking of the way back through time; Eskeleth itself was a few miles up the dale, as near as it was in his time, but far off in years.

'I hev ti git mysen thruff,' he said. Through, he meant. 'I've been in ivery lead-working and hoil in t'grund, and niver found a way. I set off on t'road here laiting of treasure, plenty of gold and that. If I could find that and get away back ti Eskeleth . . .' He shook his head. 'I will,' he said. 'I will. Who wants to be here?'

However, he looked round the warm café, took a slurp of tea, and seemed to be settled in. He is just feeling life, Keith thought. He'll get used to it.

'You never will get back there,' said David. 'If you'd found the treasure and got back to your own time, then we would have heard of you. We haven't heard of you.'

'We might have heard,' said Keith. 'But it's like hag-worms to us and we don't believe it.'

'The like of that,' said John. 'I do it, in a week, happen, and get home rich, and you don't hear of me, I'm so rich I'm a lord and get another name. Then thou's heard of me and not known, David. Me and Kath, eh, Lord Mayor? I'll be right yet.'

He finished his tea, buttoned up his coat, and said he was off, there was milking yet, and he had to walk to Swang. Frank Watson thought that his visits to York should not take the place of work.

'We're just having a plate of chips,' said David. 'If Keith has any money.'

'Nay, I's off,' said Nellie Jack John. He stood up and made his way towards the door. He had to wait there a moment while someone else came in. Keith took all the money that David had, found some of his own, and went to the counter for the chips.

When he got to the table with them David said, 'What's Nellie Jack John doing? First he didn't go out, and now he's gauping through the window.'

Through the steam on the glass Nellie Jack John could be seen cloudily, wrapped in his coat, staring.

David waved the plate of chips at him. 'Come in, you daft beggar,' he said. Nellie Jack John could not hear, of course, and was not looking in David's direction.

90

'I'll get him,' said Keith. But Nellie Jack John turned away then, and was off. Keith at the door saw him walking steadily away.

'That night,' said David. 'That other night.'

'It was all right,' said Keith. He fingered his scab. It was not yet ripe. He ate a chip instead. Giving up scabs is much more serious than giving up sweets.

'It was terrible,' said David. 'You don't know.'

'I don't understand where it came from,' said Keith. 'I nearly got a clue the other night, but I can't remember what it was. I fell asleep.'

'Time-warps are simple,' said David. 'There might be parallel universes where everything is the same until a certain point and then things go in different ways. But if one of them doesn't quite separate, then you would get things going wrong without being able to understand why.'

'Then there's a lot of parallel universes,' said Keith. 'Look at everything that goes wrong.'

'Just wipe the table down,' said David, using paper napkins. He had something in mind. 'Something might come back to you. At first I was only going to kill you, because you must have stolen him from the hospital. Then I was going to do much worse things because you must have taken him from, you know, St Agatha's.'

'I didn't know St Agatha's,' said Keith. 'I never heard of the mouse.'

'You couldn't have done either,' said David. 'It just felt possible and it must have been one of them. But it can't have been, so we don't know what it was. If you see him again you might remember. Did you know he could run about and not fall off tables?'

'You showed me,' said Keith. 'The other night.'

'I knew it couldn't be your fault,' said David. 'But somebody knows.'

'It might not be their fault either,' said Keith.

'You don't half have stinky pockets,' said David, reaching into one of his.

'Mum didn't like to wash him,' said Keith; and as he said it David was looking disappointed and pained because of being told pointless lies.

'No, no,' said Keith. 'It was in my pocket when my mum washed the coat, so she took it out and put it back later. But I still don't know how it got there at all.'

'I just want to know,' said David. Keith gave him the history of the shooting coat, which he was wearing at that moment. 'Gun oil,' he said, showing a stain. 'Bonfire night burn. Paint from when he fell off the ladder. When I inherited it the pockets were empty. It wasn't new.' New clothes had a coin in the pocket for luck.

David brought Muz out and held him. Muz had bead eyes. Muz had his tail in place.

'Superglue,' said David. Muz wagged the tail.

'People will see,' said Keith.

'Move the plate,' said David, winding Muz. 'No one will notice.'

Muz scampered about the table. He was running better now. 'Oiled,' said David. 'Engine was full of fluff.' Muz swung to a stop, twitched, and fell over on his side. 'D' said his belly label. An eye reflected bars of fluorescent light.

Keith held out the last charred chip. Muz ignored it. 'Be like that,' said Keith.

It mattered, and it did not matter. If Muz had eaten the chip that would have been more perfect than was necessary. For Keith to offer it, for David to allow it to be offered, showed that the fight was forgotten, that though the reasons could not be known, no one was to blame.

But Muz now moved. Muz moved backwards.

His tail hung over the edge of the table and was being pulled.

A small hand had taken hold. A child was standing there and removing him. She looked at Muz. She looked at Keith.

David was amused. He was protective too. His hand was ready to snatch Muz back into ownership.

The child had a similar idea. She ignored David.

'Muz,' she said. She said it to Keith, explaining the name of the mouse to him. Her sparkly pink glasses reflected, like Muz's eye, the tubes of light overhead. Her hand now closed on Muz. 'Davy,' she said, but still to Keith. Her voice was husky but her words clear.

David was leaning forward, ready to get Muz back, because he was not going to part with him, yet did not seriously think he would lose him. He was looking round for the owner of the child.

The child held Keith's chair with one hand. She stood crooked, her legs uncomfortable. She had a small frown of thoughtfulness and purpose.

'Muz belongs to me now, Davy,' she said.

'Not me,' said Keith.

'It's got D on it,' said the child, turning Muz over, showing his label.

'Get it off her,' said David. 'What are you doing?'

'I'm not doing anything,' said Keith. 'She thinks I'm you.'

'Davy,' said the child.

Keith was now being put in the wrong again, without knowing how it could be so. Davy was not his name; he was not allowed to use it on David; he had never owned Muz.

But he had seen this child several times: at the Bowlorama, and in the market place.

'The shoe-counter,' he said, going straight to the earliest meeting, which David had shared.

'Who is it?' asked David. 'What's your name?' he said to the child.

She looked round. She had to turn her whole body round to do

93

so, which she did stiffly, backing in a half circle because she still held Keith's chair with one hand.

Billy was two tables away, her hair scraped back, quite unlike her shoe-counter appearance. She was talking to the waitress gathering trays. She did not notice the child looking at her. She wore the doggy-fur coat, black fading to grey.

The child was thinking. She turned herself towards the boys again. 'Busy,' she said, explaining Billy. She paused then and thought. She was thinking about her name, it seemed. At last she said it. 'Clare,' she said. 'D was for Donna.' She told Keith, not David.

David said, 'She's obviously lost. We'd better give her to someone. Who do you belong to?' he asked her. 'We'll get you back.'

The child looked at him. She had no interest in what he was saying, but responded politely as she had before, looking back towards Billy. This time Billy was looking back and gave her an encouraging smile, and then, ignoring David as the child did, gave Keith a friendly nod, which meant something like, I am glad you two have become acquainted and please carry on making friends. It was addressed to Keith and to the child.

'I belong to Davy,' said the child.

'It's time we went,' said Keith, overwhelmed with strangeness, feeling that one part of his mind was seeing reality and another part running a confused dream, wondering how he had become concussed without knowing anything about it.

'Best,' said David. 'But my . . .' He was pushing his chair back, getting up, reaching out his hand for Muz, and the child was pulling her hand away.

At that moment the waitress came with a tray, plonked it down, lifted two mugs of tea from it, and took away the chip plate. 'Lady over there,' she said, nodding her head. 'Sent you these.'

The lady over there was Billy, who smiled at them both.

'I think we'd better go,' said David, at once. 'I don't know these people. Get my mouse for me.'

Keith laid out his open hand. The child put the mouse on it. 'Goodbye,' said Keith, and stood up as David stood.

They left quickly. David was saying, 'This doesn't happen in England.' They got to the door, and it opened on them. Nellie Jack John came in, carrying a cloud of cold with him, looking round the room, coughing a little on the steam and smoke, blinking at the coarse light.

His eyes focused. 'I'd to come away back,' he said. 'By.' His last word was an expression of admiration. He was staring at Billy. 'It's our Kath all ower agen. Now David, thou gan and tell her I's courting and that I think she's a real grand lass, and there'll come a time.'

'We're going,' said Keith.

'You're too late,' said David. 'She's taken a fancy to Keith. Something has gone wrong with the parallel universe.'

'Well, wilt'a tell her?' said Nellie Jack John.

'I'm just going home,' said David. 'I don't like it here, and Keith never understands anything.' He was half joking and half serious. Keith felt his arm tense and trembling against him.

'But now you know what it's like, not understanding,' said Keith. 'I don't know what's going on at all. None of it's anything to do with me.'

'Then I'll ha' to frame alone,' said Nellie Jack John. 'But wait on, eh?'

The child had now gone back to Billy. Nellie Jack John drew himself up straight and soldierly. His hands looked for drumsticks. He drew a breath and walked across the café towards Billy.

'We'll have that tea,' said Keith. 'And get away any time. They think they know us but they don't.'

95

'If she's a town girl,' said David, sitting down again, 'then she might be descended from John's Kath and look like her.'

'She must be quite old,' said Keith.

'She hasn't lived since then,' said David. 'Unless she followed him through the time-warp.'

Keith thought that if so she might lead him back.

'How did she get Muz?' David wondered. 'Why did she get my name and then give it to an ugly idiot? And why . . . ?'

'Why what?' asked Keith.

'That kid says her name is Donna,' said David. 'And that the D on Muz is for that. She also says her name is Clare. But the D on Muz is for me.'

'Yes,' said Keith. David had recited fact. Nellie Jack John was now sitting at Billy's table. The little girl was crayoning in a book.

'And she says Muz belongs to you, but she thinks you are Davy. She thinks you are me. It fits together exactly,' said David.

'What do you mean, fits together?' said Keith. 'It simply doesn't mean anything.'

David looked at him. 'I won't say,' he said. 'I must be wrong. What's Nellie Jack John doing?'

'Drinking tea,' said Keith. 'Standing up. He isn't right pleased.'

Nellie Jack John came over with his tea and sat down. He was not pleased. 'By Gow, they mannish different these times,' he said. 'Sha wean't say owt ner nowt. I doubt she doesn't rightly ken what I said. I told her I niver minded t'calf at foot. I'll ha' to ask again another year.' He swallowed his tea, wiped his lips, nodded to Billy, and began to march out. In three paces he turned. 'She says, which of you is't?' Then he was outside again.

'Which of us is what?' asked Keith.

'Then it is that,' said David. 'What am I going to do? I'm used to how it was. Don't you see?'

Keith shook his head slowly. At Billy's table the child pushed her glasses up, looked across the café, and said, 'Mams, I like the other one best.'

'She doesn't like you, Keith,' said David. 'It's instinct. The time-warp is still here, and everything fits all the way if you know the baby's name. Mum and I knew and we never told anyone. If it was a girl she was to be called Clare. Clare Wix. I think that must be her, my sister.'

XIII

'You'll have to make the best of it,' David had said next. 'It isn't a matter of choice.'

Keith had walked out of the café then. There and then, he thought, getting up with half a mug of tea left on the table wanting to be drunk, going out, and setting off home. He had had no idea of what he thought. He had hardly any idea where he was going, only that home was at the end of it.

Being jumped on and thumped by David was painless and without consequence, compared with being thrown right out of David's life with those few words about having no choice.

He went round by the castle, down to the river, across the bridge, up the hill, finding far-distant foreign country ahead. He turned, came down again, and walked the edges of town until it felt like midnight, but the church clock only rang eight.

Keith did not mind that David was preferred and liked better; that was David's due, and Keith would take second place to him in anyone's opinion.

But to be told there was no choice about being given second place by David himself was more than he would let anyone see he was thinking about. He preferred the dark.

It might not be second place; in fact it must be a long way below second place if you counted family, David's father, mother, or sister.

It could not be a sister, Keith thought. It could not be any sister brought back from not being born alive. It could not be that one, that mother.

David was waiting beside Keith's door, about a quarter past eight.

'I didn't know which way you would come home,' he said. 'But I knew you would. So I got here first. Logic.'

Keith looked at the fuzzy reflection of a streetlamp in the shiny door. His hands were yellow with its light.

'Great piece of programming,' said Keith, analysing the fuzziness of the light. Something causes it, he thought. Brush strokes in the paint. Holograms. There isn't a single bit of the picture in exactly the right place, but it comes out so we know what it is. It is a hundred per cent wrong, and ninety per cent right. 'Do you want to come in. What about them?'

'Don't know,' said David. 'When I got out you'd gone so I came on down here. I'm sick with cold.'

'I'm sick with you,' said Keith.

When they got into the house Mrs Heseltine disregarded Keith and asked only how David was, just looking at Keith so that David knew the scab on his cheekbone was being considered.

'I'm all right,' said David. 'I won.'

'Oh yes, dear,' said Mrs Heseltine, going back to her letter-writing, not getting the right answer.

'Mrs Heseltine,' said David. 'Please tell me about Muz.'

'Muz who?' she asked. 'I say Mrs or Miss, or Dame or Lady, whatever it happens to be; or Mayoress, or Highness. But never Ms. The rules are quite clear, even if I have to look them up. Your Grace, for instance, is sometimes right.'

'M, U, Z,' said David, drawing Muz from his pocket.

'You are quite cold,' said Mrs Heseltine. 'You hands are blue and your nose is dripping.'

'Muz,' said David, holding him up in one hand, extending the tail with the other. 'Do you want to see him work.'

'I didn't know his name,' said Mrs Heseltine.

'But you put it in Keith's pocket,' said David.

'Yes,' said Keith. 'You said so.'

'I found it there,' said Mrs Heseltine. 'The same as I found four melted sweets in his trouser pocket after they had been washed.'

'Oh,' said Keith, 'I know what happened.'

'Green, red, yellow, and black,' said his mother. 'I thought they were caterpillars again. You'll have to ask Keith about the mouse.'

'Yes,' said Keith. 'I know now.'

'Or Your Majesty,' said Mrs Heseltine, because now no one was listening to her she could daydream.

'It was the day the boggart threw pig-muck at us,' said Keith, in his own room. 'I met some kids from the primary school outside the sweet shop, and they gave me the ones in my trouser pocket. Then this kid, that one, you know, Donna.'

'Clare,' said David.

'No,' said Keith. 'Donna. You're talking nonsense. But she was crossing to their car, the blue one with flames on the front, and she held on to my coat. She can't walk so well.'

'Jinky-backed,' said David. 'Nellie Jack John says. Lambs get it.'

'And she got hold of my coat,' said Keith. She put it in my pocket then, she must have been the one, and I came home and hung the coat out the back because they wouldn't have it in the house. And that's why it's there.'

David was rubbing his wrists together, with some theory about getting warm quicker that way. 'I knew there was a link,' he said.

'But she isn't your sister,' said Keith. 'And I'm not going to have no choice about making the best of it. I just don't believe it.'

Muz ran about a table. He was so excited he miscalculated a corner and fell off.

'See,' said Keith. 'It doesn't even work.'

'Cold,' said David. 'I waited out there to say something different. Your link just makes it more certain. There must be a link back to my mum.'

' "Another inch round the equator," ' said Keith. 'He wrote that.'

'Because she had Muz,' said David. 'On the table beside her bed, But not the box or the key. I thought you had taken him, but you couldn't.

'No,' said Keith. 'If you'd thought about it.'

'If I'd thought,' said David. 'Did it hurt?'

'I couldn't pittle for ages,' said Keith.

'Do you want him for a bit?' said David, holding out Muz. It was his best way of being sorry.

Keith stroked Muz. 'He's a good man,' he said. 'It's the master that's a barmpot. You've got an idea working in your head and it's foaming over all wrong. Thou's a barmpot.'

'A,' said David, listing what he had to say, 'how did Clare . . .'

'Donna,' said Keith.

' . . . know my name?' David continued. 'B, how did she knows Muz's name? C, she is the right age. She was born on the 9th of July, and I know her age unto the hour, like that nurse in the play. I asked after you left. D, how could she have Muz?'

'Time-warp,' said Keith. 'It's not proved.' And of course the play had not worked for anyone – merely a messy tragedy, no one sensible.

'Of course not,' said David. 'But if it's right I can't simply do nothing. I've got to make the best of it, and so have you. We haven't got the choice of doing nothing. You wouldn't do nothing if it might be your flesh and blood, your own mother's child.'

'I do everything I can for myself,' Keith agreed. 'I don't believe half of what I think, but I am my own mother's child, so I make the best of that. But you should ask your dad.'

'I don't believe it as much as that,' said David. 'I do want to because I did have a sister. And I don't want to because it isn't the one I would choose at all.'

'He would know,' said Keith. 'Your dad.' It was tragedy if Clare wasn't his sister, and tragedy if she was; but at least he could not be in love with her. And just at that moment, interrupting the conversation, the thought came to him that Dr Wix was . . . But David was speaking, though of course not about Juliet.

'He can't if we don't tell him,' said David, and shouting, 'are you listening, ugly idiot? But if I have a sister I have to do something about it. That's the only choice.'

'I shall just walk straight past,' said Keith. 'They are making you believe.' . . . With Sister Mackenzie. And David did not want to know, or dare not hope; and Donna, or Clare, was a diversion from making up his mind.

'I said we'd go up,' said David. Not Romeo speaking.

'Where?' said Keith, not catching up with David at once. But he knew before David told him. And of course other things were explained and there were things David had not been doing. It was a step forward, but from a step already back, an energetic standstill.

'I need you to be with me,' said David. 'Just in case I am a barmpot. Unless you can think of some other way to explain what happened.'

'Didn't happen,' said Keith, sulkily. 'OK.'

Muz paraded the table again. Mrs Heseltine came in and watched.

'There's nothing like a drop of poison for vermin,' she said. 'I didn't know he did that.'

'He prefers chips,' said Keith.

XIV

Nellie Jack John would not come with them to where Billy lived.

'I've found another spot to look at,' he said. 'And what for would I want to speak with her? There's nowt going off in that airt. I's off to find a road back heeam and my own folk.'

Besides, he said, he'd been on that morning and left milk and a few of sticks and coals.

David and Keith followed his tracks from Swang Farm and up the hill to the Shooting Box.

Keith was concerned about people living in the building, where they had no right to be. David was more interested in the history of the child.

'It's no worse than my shed at home,' he said. 'I just want to know how it's my sister. Even if it's time-warp stuff the logic has to be there.'

'If it is,' said Keith, against the idea. 'There's different things to do if it is, or if it isn't.'

'It won't be so simple,' said David. 'It hasn't been so far.'

'You never found you had just a car to live in,' said Billy, when they were in the building. 'Nothing else. I knew this spot, but we're still living in the car.'

That room of the Shooting Box was warm. The fire was stacked high in the grate and a kettle hung on the crane over it.

'Just a play-house, really,' said Billy. 'I'm a Garebrough lass, you know. I played here when I was little – how I knew where to come now. I didn't break the lock. It was always broken. This . . . it's home, if it could be got right.'

There was nowhere to sit in this home. The little girl was tucked up in a wiry folding bed, asleep. She had been eating chocolate and her face was bemired with it. Her glasses were on a corner of the window bottom, looking out from a small shoe-box, its lid set up as the head of a doll's bed with a pillow and blanket. On the bedhead was written 'Muz'. Glasses slumbered there now. At the other corner a gas storm lantern with a mantle glowed softly.

Here hung the low star below the hilltop.

She is very ugly, thought Keith, looking at the child. This is all ugly. The fire hasn't started to hot the place through. It smells damp. The kid smells dirty.

He was uncomfortable because things should not be like this, and he felt he was to blame.

'It isn't ever going to be right,' said Billy. 'I can't get it right or make it right, but you've just got to carry on, haven't you?'

'People can get a house,' said Keith. 'Something. There are agencies. My dad would know. You can get money. Support.'

'I'm working,' said Billy. 'If I start getting help they'll take her away. So I don't. I keep myself. I keep her. It's just that my mam's gone into residence and she hasn't her flat any more, so she can't keep Donna. Clare.'

The child was sometimes Donna, sometimes Clare.

'My mam,' said Billy. 'She wanted to call her Donna, but I knew it was Clare.'

'It was,' said David.

'Of course I knew,' said Billy.

This isn't true, Keith was thinking. It is a fairy tale. She is making up the meaning by saying something not quite like the truth. It is going to be magic any minute. But he did not know how to tackle the question and put matters straight.

'You don't know that,' he said to David.

'I do,' said David.

'I know,' said Billy. 'She's mine.' Then she fussed with the fire for a moment. 'She's mine now,' she said.

There is a difference, Keith thought. I don't believe her. She doesn't believe herself. But David does not want to be right, only certain.

'You're cold,' Billy said to David. 'Shaking. Come next to the fire.'

'Not cold,' said David. 'I just want to know.'

'You don't,' said Keith. Partly he thought that there would be no truth. Partly he feared that David might become wild again. Because . . .

Because came next; the story if not the truth.

'I got married straight out of school,' said Billy. 'That Tate, he told me I was wrong plenty of times. But he had to call me Mrs Rattray the last week of term. Rat isn't about now, not Rattray. He didn't care about the baby after all. Tate said he wouldn't. Mam said he wouldn't. He came to see me at Monks', did Tate. Rattray didn't. I waited for him that day, but he was off. Off ever since.'

'July the 9th,' said David. 'That day.'

'I'd left school a year,' said Billy. 'Some of them still there at their desks, yes Miss, no Miss, and me married and in the Monks' Infirmary and the baby coming. Ooh, I wanted that more than anything that ever existed. It doesn't matter what. It doesn't matter what.'

She bent over the child and tucked the covers round her. The child opened her eyes and looked at them. Then she was asleep again.

'So you had her,' said Keith, thinking that that is what happens at the Monks' Infirmary. It had happened to him.

'It must be different,' said David. 'Logically.'

Keith wanted to explain that it must be different, that some other story had come into existence, that it was not a lie, though it sounded like one, but an attempt to answer difficult questions without making a difference to truth. But by the time he had thought about calling it out loud a plausible lie the moment had passed.

Billy was going on. She had practised saying the next part, Keith was sure. It sounded as if she was reading the few words out.

'It was my baby in the next room,' said Billy. 'It really was, poor lady. I took hers. She . . .'

David stared at the fire. He turned his head and looked at the child.

'I wanted it so much,' said Billy. 'I loved her so much. I still do. She's all I've got. The little gobbet of snot.'

'And Muz,' said David.

'I heard you talking in there,' said Billy. 'The next room in the Infirmary. But it isn't right, is it? She's not mine.'

'She is, now,' said Keith. 'You said.'

'You ask her,' said Billy. 'I'll get her sat up. She's got this thing with her back. She's been that much in and out of the hospital that she's sickened with it, and my mam's had her between times, and here she is and I don't know how to look after her, so it's time she was nearer where she belongs. Clare, sit up. Tell them you are.'

She hung the glasses on Clare's face.

Clare looked at them. She dismissed Keith: he did not satisfy her standards. She looked at David. She likes the other one better, Keith remembered.

'I haven't got a dad,' said Clare. Her voice was little, high, exact, and piping. She was playing with a complicated torch that showed green on David's face, red on Keith's. 'She had Rattray for a bit, but he sodded off, so I haven't anyone. I'm just Davy's sister.'

'And Muz came with her,' said Billy. 'He lives in that bed. Shoe-box. I thought we'd have to live in there with him until I remembered this spot.'

'I don't know what to do,' said David, looking round this unlikely home.

'I do,' said Keith. 'We have to go now,' he told Billy. He did not want to speak with the child. 'We'll think of something.'

Outside, with a wind puckering their cheeks, David said, 'You don't mean that. Think of something.'

'You can't say you won't,' said Keith. 'And you might.'

'OK,' said David. 'If it's not true, what do we do? I don't just mean thinking of something, but doing something. And if it is true, what do we do?'

'Try to think of the right question,' said Keith.

'I'll just know the answer when it comes,' said David. 'That's all.'

On the wind a few late snowflakes helicoptered down and joined a helter-skelter across the moor.

XV

Another day snow was falling. Cars went past with their wheels muffled. Snow creaked underfoot when it was trodden on. Now and then there was a fistful of wind banging through the sky of snow, whirling flakes into a frenzy, but not altering the density.

'There's been lightning,' said David. 'It's a thaw coming. It's the end of winter.'

They were indoors. Winter was not over outdoors. David brought out a letter.

Dear Davy, it read, *Well, it seems that we shall know sooner rather than later whether the New Addition is to be a chap or a woman. Mummy saw her doctor today, between them they've arranged for her to go into the Monks' Infirmary at once, or actually yesterday, just to keep an eye on things. It has gone midnight now, because I have been cooking my own supper. I had to eat it for myself, too. It was two lamb chops, a handful of new potatoes, eleven leaves of mint, and 167 green peas, followed by eight strawberries, one cream, and 4,328 grains of sugar. I know you have enjoyed today, four lumps of gristle, five well-boiled leaves of cabbage, eleven lumps of smashed potato, four currants (for the whole school) in a pudding (boiled in the cook's socks) and huge helpings of the world-famous diseased custard (for which no cure has been found, or even a recipe).*

The fact is that Mummy and I can't come over together on Saturday, which you probably know by now. But I shall come on Friday evening and bring you back home until Sunday evening.

I hope you are thinking of names. If it is a boy we shall call it Handful, after the potatoes, and if it is a girl we shall call it Gristle.

Mummy says she is feeling tremendous. She probably means huge! With love, Dad.

'These letters come in order,' said Keith. 'You must have looked. You are reading them.'

'Only the postmarks,' said David. 'I don't remember the words, only the feeling. It's like a taste in my mouth, all that time.'

'He was thinking of ridiculous names,' said Keith.

'Mummy and I thought of better ones,' said David. 'Robin for a boy. And it was Clare for a girl.'

He took the letter from Keith, folded it into its envelope, and put it in the drawer with the rest.

'You don't want a sister now,' said Keith.

'I wanted one then,' said David. 'We all did. I expect a boy would have been all right, but we wanted a girl. A sister.'

'You don't,' said Keith. 'I've seen people's sisters. They're nowt. Primary school is full of them.'

David considered what Keith had said, seriously. He saw what Keith meant. 'I only wanted one,' he said. 'Not the race, or species, not even the family.'

'Not even one,' said Keith. 'If that's it, brought up by wild animals.'

'I know,' said David. 'But because you don't want something doesn't mean it's not it. Or because it's not how you would like it you can't just forget it. You can't prove it's not her, and I can't prove it is.'

'It's what you set out to do,' said Keith. 'It's what Billy set out to do. You're fooling yourself. She's fooling you.'

'You've only just thought of that,' said David. 'It doesn't mean anything to you. But I thought of it on July the 9th that year. Well, I thought of it before that. What's illogical for you can be logical for me. We were going to call her Strawberry, or something.'

'Gristle,' said Keith.

'You know how he is,' said David. 'How he was.'

The sky was dense with snow all night. The random puffs of wind gathered together and brought on spasms of blizzard, now burying the cobbles in the market place, now baring them and trying to lift them. Before it dropped towards evening, two buses had kissed each other's backsides on the slope. The caption of the picture in the paper of the buses read, 'Hands, knees, and . . .'

The curves on overhead electric and telephone cables were influenced horizontal by the wind and abandoned gravity. Someone in Keith's class said the wires were being sentimental.

Frank Watson was not being sentimental. The wind had carried away his telephone wires. He had to come into the town for Nellie Jack John.

'This is the last time,' he was saying to Mrs Heseltine. 'I'll ha' no more on't. If he wants to be up and away as he pleases he can have his time back and not be behoven to me.'

'He hasn't been here, Frank,' said Mrs Heseltine. 'Has he, Keith?'

'He'll be on the hill somewhere,' said Keith. 'It's his own time he's looking for, Frank.'

'It's my time he's living on,' said Frank. 'I'll go up by David's and see there.'

'I'll get my coat and come on with you,' said Keith.

In the still air the Land-Rover was surrounded by its own fumes, brownish-blue and oily.

'On the hill?' said Frank, driving off and leaving the shroud of smoke like a ghost.

'Looking for the way back,' said Keith.

'The poor silly lad,' said Frank. 'He should be heafed in by now, content with his pasture. There isn't any way back.'

'There was a way here,' said Keith. But Frank could not see that as a fact.

'Whatever,' he said. 'It's a big hill to lie out on with a broken leg. And it'd best be broken before he lands home, or I'll crack the other one and all.' He was making a joke.

Nellie Jack John was not at David's house.

'I'd best be back and looking,' said Frank. 'I'm ready to call him,' (he meant scold), 'but he's to be found first.'

'We'll come up with you,' said David. 'Sister Mackenzie, tell my dad we're off to Swang.'

'Sister,' said Keith.

'Idiot,' said David.

'And tell my mum,' said Keith.

'Cover your heids,' said Sister Mackenzie, as they went out to the Land-Rover.

'A right sensible lad, otherhands,' Frank said. 'Just saying last night how it needs a snow again to take the last lot away. This isn't fit to be out in.' Outside the town the snow had drifted from gateways a foot and more deep, tapering across the road. 'You'd best get out and walk back now, you two.'

'He's our responsibility,' said David.

Nellie Jack John was at Swang when they got there.

'Gone out to fodder and that,' said Eileen. 'You lads come in. Frank will drop you back in a bit. Isn't the weather bad?'

'Come in, Keith,' said David. Frank was going out to have his say with Nellie Jack John.

'He'll just shout and that,' said Eileen. 'Wondering whether help's worth the trouble. You know how he is. He always wanted a lad, and now he has one and he wants to rear him right. But too much playing war and the boggart wakes up and there's mischief.'

114

Frank came back with Nellie Jack John. 'I got right lost,' said Nellie Jack John. 'I've had no dinner, no bait, and no tea. There's water running under. I was fast under a rock, and bangled and belantered, and I came out and I's here yet, so I haven't gitten anywheer.'

'We'll all have some tea, Mother,' said Frank.

'I used to hate to be called that,' said Eileen. 'But it's better than my own name now.' Nellie Jack John bowed his head as she went past, and she ruffled his hair.

'You're home, lad,' said Frank. 'Bar the shouting.'

After the pot of tea Frank took David and Keith to the end of the track, turned round, and went back to the farm. His headlamps turned a triangle of snow translucent and yellow, getting smaller and smaller in the shapeless countryside, seeming to get further away.

After that there was darkness, in spite of the whiteness of the snow. Invisible sources of light were filling local and distant horizons.

There was no traffic. The most recent tracks round the bridge over Jingle Beck were still the Land-Rover's. Down below, in this inapprehensible quarterlight, Jingle Beck itself had become smooth under snow. Beneath it, water was audibly moving.

They pulled up the further bank, beginning to hear traffic. A vehicle was banging its way through the drifts, wheels sometimes spinning, then catching, and coming nearer.

At the top of the slope the road went to the right for the town. Straight on was the small track to the Shooting Box. The struggling vehicle was coming downhill, apparently digging its way through with the light from its lamps.

'Let's go back to Swang,' said Keith. 'And start out again later.'

But as they watched, the car came to the exit of the track and stopped completely, its wheels spinning, climbing and dropping back from the ridge pushed up by a passing snow-plough.

'We'll have to help,' said David.

'I know,' said Keith. 'It's what you believe, David, so just believe in nonsense if you like. Just get her through and be on our way.'

'But,' said David, 'your "if" is at the end of what you say; mine is right at the beginning.'

They began to kick snow down in front of the car, and to pull it away by hand.

Billy wound down her window and put her head out.

'I've got to be away,' she said. 'I have. Help me out on the road and I'll be right.' Then she saw clearly who it was. 'Oh,' she said, 'You don't know what it's like up there. I don't know what it is, but it's terrible, terrible noises, walking through the house, in the walls, up the floor, I just came out. I put her in the car first off and went back in, but I couldn't get all the gear. I don't know what to do. Don't go up there, there's something banging and shaking, God, I was frightened. I thought it was snow, but it was in the room with me. Listen, I've got summat for you. I was going to drop it off at the house, but I'll get it out now. I don't know what else to do. I've taken hours to get down in this sodding snow. I'll be late for work again and get laid off. I'll be back for it.'

While they dug she opened the back of the car and brought things out. At a last kick of snow the front wheels dropped to tarmac.

Billy dropped the hatch down and got into the car again. 'Look after it,' she said. 'You'll know what to do.'

Then she was battling her way along the road, swerving round drifts.

'It'll be nothing,' said Keith. They were both blinking in new darkness. Billy had left a heap of some sort in the mouth of the track, like a bundle of rugs.

'We don't want any of her muck,' said Keith, thinking of tea-bags and orange peel and other slight rubbish thrown out on the hillside. 'Why didn't she give us a ride on?' He batted his hands together. They were wet, cold, and glowing.

'She's got frightened by something up there,' said David. 'What could she leave?'

It could be anything, Keith thought. She could have come across anything on the moor; anything, walking in walls, up the floor. 'Rubbish collection tomorrow,' he said.

'They'll take it.'

'She's gone,' said David. 'It's better. I can forget it all. I was going to anyway.'

'Well done, thou good and ham-fisted bucket of worms,' said Keith.

The bundle on the snow flashed a point of white light, of green light, of red light.

'Take me home, Davy,' it said.

XVI

'What is it?' said Eileen, when the sledge came into her kitchen, its runners scraping over the threshford and grating on the flags. 'It's looking at me.'

'My dad made that 'boggan when I was a lad,' said Frank. 'It's a lang 'un to hold all five of us lile lads.'

'Oh Frank,' said Eileen, seeing the load it carried. 'What is it? What have these boys done?'

Nellie Jack John heard the scraping and came out of the room to look. 'She sent it back,' he said. Then the bundle looked at him too. 'By Gow,' he said, and went back into the room.

David had said, at the place where track and road met, 'We can't leave it here.'

The talking bundle had been laid the length of the sledge. But more than that was difficult to make out in this night; only that there was an interruption to the pallid gleam of snow.

'If I was alone I wouldn't have seen it,' Keith had said. 'Would I?'

'Of course you would,' said David. 'But you wouldn't have known what to do next and you'd both be loaded into the dustcart tomorrow morning. But we've got to do something now, and that is take it to Swang.'

'Policeman,' said Keith, thinking officially, the easy way.

'They'd just put it in a household,' said David. 'So we'll do the same.'

'Home,' said the bundle.

'It'll be a nice place,' said David.

Keith was pondering slowly the point that the child was meant to be at David's house, if anyone believed the mother. 'But,' he said, wondering what he might say and finding nothing.

'It's the only place,' said David.

So it had been a long pull round by Jingle Beck, half a mile to the track, and a mile along that, and round to the yard door at Swang.

Along the way they had told the package on the sledge where she was going.

'It's my cousin,' Keith had said.

'It's my brother,' said the child.

'It's a farm,' said David. 'You'll like that.'

The child had said, 'My feets are cold.' Keith had tucked a hairy rug round a small bare foot that was like marble. There was something colder and harder than that round the ankle.

David was pulling the rope. Keith pushed at the back of the sledge, keeping it in the raised centre of the track. The axles of the Land-Rover had smoothed that part down and left it high. The wheel ruts to either side were filling as they walked.

As they went the night bit down harder and the cold snow skinned over with frost.

At Swang they opened the door and pushed the sledge into the kitchen without knocking.

'So what is it?' Eileen was now asking again.

The bundle was no longer visibly looking at her, because its glasses had steamed up. Eileen came forward and pulled them away.

'It's a little lass,' she said. 'Well, I don't understand that.'

'It might be summat else,' said Frank. 'More of them crawling through from the back of history, two hundred years.'

120

'Seven years,' said David. 'Out of history.'

'History is real,' said Keith. 'That bit is a story.'

Eileen was unwrapping the bundle now. Frank was talking about other things they'd had enough of. 'Worse things,' he said.

'Clap cold,' Eileen was saying about the child in the bundle. 'Well, this is no sort of a way to be. What's your name?'

The child looked at her, at David, and at Eileen again. Her lips moved but she did not speak.

'Found it by the road,' said Keith. He hoped she would not cry. She decided not to.

'The light's funny,' said David, in a bothered voice. 'Rainbowy.' He pointed to the floor. 'Just there.'

At that moment something ran from 'just there' across the flags. It left damp traces, but could not itself be seen.

'I can see it,' said David, blinking. 'Sparkly.'

'It's called Donna,' said Keith. He did not mean the thing running on the flagstones.

'Now sit up, Donna,' said Eileen, wanting to take her from the bundle.

'Clare,' said the child. She was now trying to lift herself up, but she had no ground she could push against on either side. However, she pulled away from Eileen, who was trying to lift her, trying to manage for herself. She had much difficulty, and was nearly in tears with helplessness.

'You're clemmed,' said Eileen. 'Frank, go and turn on the bath but don't run it right hot. About for a baby would do.'

'We haven't had a baby,' said Frank. 'What would you like it at? Churning heat? The dairy thermometer has that on.'

'Aye, that,' said Eileen. 'Now you're coming up, Clare, like or not. Give me your hands.'

However, Clare had something else for her hands to do. She was now patting what was perched on her, pleased and smiling with her pet.

'You know what yon is on the floor?' said Frank, pointing with the dairy thermometer, half a yard of brass tube with graduated glass along it.

'It's the boggart,' said Eileen. 'I hope, boggart, you're the right end out.'

'He's happy,' said David. 'Keith, it runs in the family.' He was able to control the Swang boggart some of the time. 'It proves it. It's genetic.'

'It doesn't prove anything,' said Keith. 'Anyone can do it. Well, people of more than one family.' The boggart had broken saucers on his head before now. But for David it had been obedient. For Clare it was apparently submissive.

Then Eileen was drawing in her breath, finding metal supports on Clare's legs. 'We'll have you warm first,' she said, lifting her and the boggart. 'And clean.' She folded the bundle closed again. 'Push that outside,' she said. 'It's to wash in the morning.'

She and her burden passed Frank on the stairs. He came down with the thermometer, frowning at the unexpected visitor. He looked about carefully, shaking his head with resignation about the boggart. Keith was closing the door after the sledge had been run out through it. Outside the yard dog was snarling at the sledge, or the wolf-like coat on it. At that moment too the boggart was against a cupboard door, and the door was rattling and vibrating.

'Scratching itself,' said David.

'But what else?' said Frank. 'I don't like to leave her alone with that out again. But I have to take you back to the town, or I don't know what you mightn't land back with before the night's out. But we'll wait while Eileen lands down, and you can tell me what you know, for you know summat.'

'Some what but not all what,' said David.

Clare, from the stairs, called out, 'Davy.'

David called back after half a second's delay, 'Goodnight.' There was a cry back, but not a word.

'Get by the fire,' said Frank. 'You're no better ner that bairn. I can feel the cold on you. I'll put the kettle on.'

In the next room Nellie Jack John was sitting at the table reading the local newspaper, inch by inch, line upon line. He looked up. 'What for did you bring it here?' he asked. 'Where at is the mother?'

'Gone,' said Keith. 'Left it at the roadside. We brought it on to put it somewhere.'

'What for?' Nellie Jack John asked again. 'That should have been necked first go off. It'll niver thrive and git to market. It's not fendable. It'll be half-rocked and a fondy and all, I doubt.'

'We couldn't leave it in the snow,' said David. 'I don't know all your words, only what you mean.'

'You weren't so fendable yourself once,' said Keith. 'We didn't leave you then.'

'Happen,' said John. 'Now, if it's here or not it won't be for long. I'm finding ways in the hill, and I'll break back through before so long. Think on, if I go back and forth.'

'But you never did,' said David.

'It's not on the paper yet,' said John, agreeing, going back to his reading, to find and to prove.

Keith thawed by the fire. David paced about, half listening to the rest of the house. Frank came in with mugs of tea.

'No harm coming to it,' he said. 'But if you were expecting nowt why did you take my 'boggan, David?'

'I didn't,' said David, looking towards Nellie Jack John.

'I lent it to it mother,' said Nellie Jack John. 'A bit back, just to get about with.'

'It got left by the roadside,' said Keith. 'Ladened with that. That's all we know, isn't it, David? Not counting guesses.'

'We'll see what Eileen has to say,' said Frank. 'She's finding a place for it for tonight. Tomorrow I don't know.'

Eileen was upstairs singing quietly. A little voice joined in an unknown song.

'Women's stuff,' said Frank, hands round a mug of tea. 'There's not been so very much baby talk in this house.'

'Nobody has any bairns these days,' said Nellie Jack John. 'All the families breed small you'd think it was plague carried them off, but first off they never had 'em.'

Eileen walked across the floor above. She closed a door and came down. She did some work at the sink and then came through, drying her hands.

'That's first aid,' she said. 'That puts her on till morning. How did you come by that, and her sorry story, David? Davy.'

'The mother just said,' said David. 'She got our names wrong at first.'

'Or she made it up,' said Keith. 'It's what the mother told her.'

'She's been in hospitals,' said Eileen. 'I was a nurse when I was a girl, and I know the scars.'

'Jinky-backed,' said Nellie Jack John.

'Just about,' said Eileen. 'But she's geyly now in herself. She says she'll stop here and . . . this sounds daft, she says the boggart will look after her. He was on the shelf. I saw the wood bending, so I told her. Best to be plain with her. She says it's a cat, or the like, and she calls it Boggy. We couldn't say our prayers. It blew out the candle.'

'We'll find who she is,' said Frank.

'I know who she is,' said Eileen. 'Her mother's looking for a house for them.'

'Not here she isn't,' said Frank. 'And they can take the boggart with them.'

'We know who she isn't, and all,' said Eileen.

124

'I said so,' said Keith.

Nellie Jack John was set to watch over Eileen and the boggart while Frank took David and Keith to the town. The trail of the sledge ran all the way down the middle of the track.

David was out first, shaking his head and saying nothing, too cold to think.

At home, Keith found his mother puzzled by an envelope that had been put through the door, addressed simply to 'Davy'.

'I suppose it means David,' she said. 'But no one calls him that now. Give it to him in the morning.' She handed over an envelope filled with a sort of paper that did not flatten easily. The word on the front was in a neat backhand. The flap on the back was very loose.

In the morning it had come open. There was one slip of white paper inside, with words on it in the same backhand, swelling and flowing and firm. They read, 'This is the children money it, i come each weak look after her til I get a place she knows she is saif I,ll be back, Billy.'

The other paper was all bank-notes, their writing mean and fussy. Of the two, Billy's could be believed, not the promises of the Bank of England.

XVII

'It's a lot of money,' said Dr Tate. He flicked the notes through his fingers, or his fingers through the notes. 'You want me to lock it in the school strong room? What's it doing at school? You are asked not to bring money or valuables.'

Keith and David were standing in front of him in the school office. There was no school strong room. Dr Tate had wanted to know what he was to take charge of. 'What is it?' he had asked, 'These days we have to be careful.'

'I don't think it's mine,' said David.

'Of course not,' said Keith. 'It's nothing to do with him.'

Dr Tate was puzzled by that. 'But, Heseltine, you brought it to school and gave it to Wix. So how can it be nothing to do with him?'

'We'll give it to Eileen,' said David.

'Of course,' said Keith.

'I don't think we have an Eileen in the school,' said Dr Tate. 'Or perhaps *she* should be asking me to look after it?'

Keith looked at David, and David looked at Keith.

'What's the story?' said Dr Tate. I see we're thinking three ways. David has some facts and some opinions; Keith has some opinions and some facts; and I have neither facts nor opinions, but one hundred and thirty five pounds of sterling, property of the Bank of England. I think we better all sit down. I'm sure you've done nothing you shouldn't, because if you had you wouldn't have come to me, I'd have come to you. But someone should hear you through, either here or at home.'

'I can't say it at home,' said David.

'I can understand,' said Dr Tate. 'There are some distractions, I hear.'

Keith thought this remark invaded privacy; and that David still could not bear the thought that his mother might be replaced by Sister Mackenzie, if he knew of the possibility. Or if Dr Wix realised it.

'It's more difficult,' said David.

'We didn't kidnap it,' said Keith.

'Good God,' said Dr Tate. 'What are you saying? Kidnap what?'

'My sister,' said David.

Keith could go back to his classes then. Half an hour later Dr Tate sent for him again.

'Do you think it is supposititious?' Dr Tate asked, in a good mood and using strange language. Keith would have asked what he meant, but had not been expecting such a monster and could only remember bits of it. Dr Tate explained. 'Now and then in history it was better to have a prince, not a princess. So if it was a princess a boy baby was sent in and exchanged, usually it is said in a warming-pan but I don't see why an attaché case would not do. That is a supposititious child.'

The attaché case was full of Mr Bazangalong's heads, Keith thought. But Bazangalong was not such a real word as Dr Tate's, so he smiled silently.

'David Wix and I, and you too, are saying nothing outside about this,' said Dr Tate. 'Dr Wix might be hurt if people imagine that he gave his own daughter away. I know it isn't so.'

'I think David is wondering about that,' said Keith. 'If he thinks it is his sister.'

'But not kidnapped by you,' said Dr Tate. 'I think you took it to the nearest house and left it to your elders to sort it out. Have you

128

any idea who the mother is? How old the child is? David knows, but he couldn't say, because it . . .'

'She,' said Keith.

'They can be he or she,' said Dr Tate, 'but quite often they are definitively it. But this one, she was born when his mother died, and he is still coming to terms with that. But I don't know how long ago. Five years?'

'Seven,' said Keith.

'And the mother? Assuming it is someone else.'

'She's called Billy,' said Keith. 'But that's not her real name. She just wears a uniform called that at the Bowlorama. But you know her, Sir. She was at this school once.'

'Billy?' said Dr Tate. 'Not under that name or in that uniform.'

'You went to see her in the Infirmary,' said Keith. 'When she was having her baby. Whichever one she had.'

'I'll have to think about that,' said Dr Tate. 'Was I carrying a warming-pan?'

He went on to say that he now knew who the mother was but information about pupils was confidential; that he felt things were a little untidy, but since the mother was an old pupil he would sort something out unofficially.

'She was a girl who dreamed several dreams at a time and then couldn't choose which to live,' he said. 'But she was always in at least one. I suppose she still is. She didn't realise she had choices but that things happened and came right and that if things went wrong you felt happier quite soon because you felt about things more deeply.'

'Yes, Sir,' said Keith, not necessarily following every turn of speech. 'The dinner bell has gone.'

'One deep calling to another,' said Dr Tate, knowing that Keith had switched off already.

★ ★ ★

'But I don't want her money,' said Eileen, holding the envelope away from her and peering into it as if the Bank of England would reach out and nip her nose with its prissy writing. She tucked the envelope behind the clock on the wall. 'Don't look at it,' she said. 'He's been in the cupboards again, and I don't know where next.'

'The boggart?' said David.

'Who else?' said Eileen. 'Mind, we've had a few in today, one way and another. There was your dad, David, we thought we should have a word with him. And we had the health visitor, and the lady from the council. I know them from fostering Nellie Jack John. Did he say anything about getting adopted?'

'He's most of the time trying to find a way back to his own time,' said Keith.

'We can't give him that,' said Eileen. 'He just wants to be sure before agreeing to be ours.'

The back door opened, and Nellie Jack John came into the kitchen beyond.

'Even without visitors it's getting a houseful,' said Eileen.

'There's fresh milk,' Nellie Jack John was saying, putting something on the worktop. 'It's stret fra' the coo and waarm. Shall I tek some on for her to sup?' He put his head round the door and saw David and Keith. 'Just to save you the trouble, like,' he said, not liking to admit he had offered to be helpful to Eileen or Clare – anything soft like that.

'I could do it,' said David at once, seeing that Nellie Jack John was the one getting the sister he had been given for himself.

'I'm sure you won't frame so well,' said Eileen. 'But you can all go. Just, if she's asleep, let her be.'

Clare was a pale face with eyes at one end of a thick eiderdown stitched into coiled sausages. She was awake. She made hardly a bulge in the pink silky cloth.

'I'm so warm,' she said.

Keith had once lain in this bed. He had not been here since. He remembered, over the next few minutes, why he had been there.

After Nellie Jack John came out of the ground he threw away a candle that had lighted his way, and Keith had recovered it later. He and David had watched its cold unquenched flame for weeks, while the candle did not shrink. By looking too closely and too often, David had been thrown out of his own time by a bolt of lightning. The same lightning had laid Keith senseless on the moor. He had been brought to this bed still did not know what he had said in the next days, but straight afterwards it had seemed foolish enough.

Now, he wondered, what was Clare thinking?

'It's a great wide bed,' she said. 'If you sit on it it makes me move about. At my last house the bed fell over if Mams sat on it. It fell over if I lied down too hard.'

'We brought drinkings,' said Nellie Jack John, holding forward a beaker of warm milk. 'I'll hold it to thy gob and thou put out thy lolliker and soss it.'

She took two or three swallows. She had a milky moustache. They did not know how to wipe it away.

'I want a book to read,' she said. 'But not a very big one. That would be too heavy. In the hospical there was a table for books.'

There was a noise outside. Someone was driving a car along the track in a bad mood, going round the house and into the yard. Then the driver was having the bad mood in the room below, saying he would never have agreed to come if he'd known he was to have his taxi knocked to pieces by snowdrifts.

'It'll be traveller to sell pig-nuts or summat of the sort,' said Nellie Jack John. 'We get forever of them, ivery month there's yan or anither.'

There were steps on the stairs. Eileen came into the room, and after her Billy, wearing a pink dress and silver shoes, her hair in stylish disarray.

'What a lot of fellows,' she said. 'Hello, rat, you've got a nice place here.'

Keith had had a dream like that in this room long ago, people remarking on its comfort without knowing what it was like to lie on the bed unable to enjoy anything. Being wildly sick, Keith recalled.

Clare was not being sick. She was entertaining guests. 'Did you find one?' she asked Billy.

'Not yet, pet,' said Billy. They greeted each other by shaking hands like strangers. But both were pleased. 'She wants a proper house.'

'I want a big bed,' said Clare.

'You have one, rat,' said Billy. 'Hey, Mr Tate sent on to the Bowlorama for me, or I'd've been at the wrong house. He got me a taxi. Rattray took my car to fettle. The man's with the farmer downstairs getting himself a coffee.'

'You got to the wrong house last night,' said Keith. 'We took that envelope to Dr Tate. That's why he came for you.'

'I's off,' said Nellie Jack John. He had been edging towards the door, not wanting to remind himself of what he once hoped of Billy.

'Don't wait round, then,' said Billy.

Eileen looked from one to another of them. 'This is a peaceful house,' she said. 'Bar when Frank does his Christmas carols. Best not argue here.'

'I'd not trouble,' said Nellie Jack John. 'I's right.' He went downstairs whistling.

'Just a child,' said Billy. 'I'm twenty-three.'

'And this one belongs to you,' said Eileen, looking at Clare.

132

'Oh no,' said Billy. 'She doesn't belong to no one. She goes her own sweet way.'

'I look after Mams,' said Clare. 'She needs it most.' She brought her hand out from under the covers and patted the eiderdown. 'Come on,' she said, but not to Billy. There was a soft thud and a depression appeared among the pink plump coils. 'Drink,' said Clare.

Keith handed her the beaker.

'Oh my God,' said Billy.

'Boggy,' said Clare, tilting the beaker above the eiderdown. The boggart drank it dry.

'Fat him up,' said Clare. 'Then we can see him.'

'You lads go down,' said Eileen. 'We'll get her up; she can't lig here all and every day. I don't know best how to put on the callipers, just. Keep an eye on the taxi-man.'

The taxi-man was uneasy out here in the country. 'But the meter's running,' he said. 'I didn't know they still had places like this.'

Some time later Eileen was coming slowly downstairs, with Billy talking away behind her. Clare walked between with a slow thud on each step.

'I'll have to get to work,' said Billy. She was explaining that some of her goods were still at the Shooting Box, but that the driver was not paid to go up the hill. 'I'm not off up there alone,' she said. They all saw the little building, distinct on the hill, its two windows dark.

'Something bad in it,' said Billy.

She shook hands again with Clare. 'There you go,' said Clare. 'Come back with a house.'

'Doesn't fuss,' said Billy. 'Be good, rat.'

David thought he and Keith might ride along with Billy to the town again. But the driver would not allow that extension.

They walked part of the way back. Not a hundred yards away the taxi had stuck with two wheels spinning. Keith went back for a garden hoe ('That's what Frank uses,' said Eileen), and scraped the drift out from underneath.

'Out here you've got to live their way,' the man grumbled. 'Better get in.'

Now on the hill the windows of the Shooting Box threw back the sunlight.

'See,' said Billy, not understanding that. 'It's in there now.'

XVIII

Sister Mackenzie's typewriter went zapata zapata pling, and a spare zapata.

'But I can't tell you about patients,' she said. Zapata, went the machine. 'And you couldn't be interested, David.' Pling.

'But he always explains about patients,' said Keith. David had not actually asked about a patient, only what a jinky-back was called if a human had it. When he saw there was to be no answer he went out into the garden, pulling on his gloves. 'The man with two heads.'

'Oh, aye,' said Sister Mackenzie. Zap, zapata pling, for the Yours sincerely line, zap, zap, zapata pling, for Richard Wix, and the letter ground out from under the roller.

'Mr Bazangalong,' said Keith. 'Had an amazing illness.'

'I've seen his card,' said Sister Mackenzie, tidying away her work. 'Away out of my office.'

The garden outside was inches deep in slush. The last snowfall was melting, but taking a long time about it. The fine crispness had turned into a dirty suspension of ice particles that slid underfoot.

David was digging a path up the steps to his shed up at the back of the garden. 'This is work for idiots,' he said, handing the shovel to Keith.

'Sister Mackenzie won't say,' said Keith. 'And no good asking Eileen. She just says it's a bad back.' The shovel slid well enough into the slush, but could then hardly be lifted out of the clinging mass, and if it came up would twist and drop the contents into the space just cleared.

'That's all we'd know if they told us the Latin,' said David. 'Bad back.'

'I think I'm catching it,' said Keith, with the shovel stuck.

They had been to Swang twice since Billy had been there, once with Dr Wix, and once when Frank had been passing with a tractor pulling a trailer.

Dr Wix had merely said his patient was coming on well, and left David and Keith to walk back. After he left, Clare had come downstairs alone.

'Leave her,' said Eileen. 'She won't thank you for helping. She's of her own mind. If she can keep up with you then you're not going fast enough. If she can't keep up then she'll struggle to a standstill. So it's no good trying to win, because that's not on.'

'So what's wrong with her?' David wanted to know.

'Jinky-backed,' said Eileen. 'Near as I can make out. You get lambs with it. But I don't know what this one would be like if there wasn't something to hold her back. If she can't go, and she tews herself trying, then she's that twined that if she was anyone else she'd get a twilt from me.'

The sneck of the room door rattled. The latch lifted, and Clare came in. 'Where is the other boy?' she asked. 'Nellie Jack John.'

'Working,' said Eileen.

'Take me sledging,' said Clare. 'But bring me back to this house. I am stopping here.'

'As long as you like,' said Eileen. 'Until your mam gets a house.'

The sledge had to have cushions put on it. The hairy coat had gone to the cleaner.

'I daredn't wash it,' Eileen had said. 'It would be like washing the wolf.'

Pulling the sledge up the fields was a numbing thing to do. It rode heavily on the damp snow and did not want to come. But it would run down gentle slopes, Clare on board with her mouth open in a one-tooth tusky grimace of joy.

She fell off at the bottom of each slope. When they took her in she was wet through and getting cold.

'You should have more sense,' said Eileen to all of them. 'Come on, you; it'll be early bed, for this is every stitch you brought with you.'

However, she was settled in a big chair for a bed by the fire. She had tea with everyone because it was four o'clocks time, when the farms do that. Frank and Nellie Jack John came in.

'My clothes are at the Shooting Box,' said Clare.

'I'll be on for them right soon,' said Nellie Jack John. 'It's just a varry busy time.'

'I'll have to stop in bed,' said Clare.

'It's a warm spot, bed,' said Nellie Jack John. 'And cheaper than buying coals. I'll git up there as soon as iver.'

When he and Frank went out David and Keith left too.

'My toes are killing me,' said Keith. Snow had leaked its iced waters into his shoes, and being by the fire had melted ice from his socks. 'I've got two left feet.'

David had two right feet, he decided. All these feet had to walk in step to the end of the track.

'They aren't any warmer,' said David. 'But we've kept them occupied.'

'That's what sisters do,' said Keith. 'Is it worth it?'

'No,' said David. 'But that isn't what it's about. I'll get used to it.'

'I shan't,' said Keith.

The next time they went up to Swang Clare was in the kitchen cooking with Eileen.

'I don't know why I'm doing all this,' she said. 'It'll never come in handy.'

'It can come in handy tomorrow,' said Eileen. 'When I'm worn out looking after you.'

'Mams doesn't know how to do these things,' said Clare. 'More butter please, Mummy. I mean Eileen. She gets food already made.'

'So long as the men get theirs ready made it'll be me that makes it,' said Eileen. 'Owt in a box is next door to nowt in a box.'

Keith knew about cooking already. He had often seen it done, he said. David had had fewer opportunities, and was happy to help. Soon he was the pupil, and Clare went to lie in front of the fire. She hurt, she said.

'She has days,' said Eileen. 'Sometimes whole ones, sometimes bits of them. But there isn't anything to give her.'

Then Clare was crying but refusing to sob. David picked her up at Eileen's request and put her into Eileen's arms. Eileen took her away.

'In about ten minutes fetch out the buns,' she said. 'The men will be in.'

David washed his hands.

In ten minutes time Nellie Jack John was in for his four o'clocks. Eileen was coming down again with stuff for the washing-machine.

'She can't help it,' she said. 'She'll have to stop in bed a bit now – I've not had the time to keep up with the last lot yet.'

'Papped herself again,' said Nellie Jack John. 'She should live in t'shippon. Folk there wouldn't notice, eh?'

'Well, if you don't get away up to the Shooting Box and bring back some gear,' said Eileen, 'then I'll have to buy for her.'

'I'll gan and lewk,' said Nellie Jack John.

He went to look a couple of days later, Eileen told Keith on the telephone, in a strange and slightly tearful way. Keith was wondering why Eileen needed to tell him, unless Nellie Jack John had fallen over and needed an ambulance. Or he had found a doorway back home. Or perhaps the boggart had become a nuisance again.

But it was something else. Nellie Jack John had had his dinner ('And it were lovely dumplings') and gone out. Eileen had seen him go, taking the sledge with him. There had been firewood on it. Eileen did not know why he thought it would be handy. He had said what he was doing. Clare had known where he was going. She had had a little sleep, then gone to the window to look up at the Shooting Box.

After a long time of quiet, Eileen had looked for her, and she was not there.

But beyond the yard were the fresh scars in the wet snow of Nellie Jack John, still with his infantryman stride, with sledgemarks ("boggan,' Eileen said). Overlying them were the shallower shuffles of someone smaller and hardly able to walk in the normal sense.

Now Keith was to come, with David, and they could catch Frank at the feed merchant's, where he had gone to pick up a bag of something and been told to wait until Keith came.

Keith telephoned David, and went to the feed merchant's himself, because that was in the middle of town and on the way.

'She's getting a trouble, is that bairn,' said Frank. 'And I've sat in the office that long he's made me pay him, so I haven't been done any good turn.'

David was waiting at home. 'It's getting late now,' he said. 'We need the rescue people.'

'We'll follow her up,' said Keith.

Keith was wondering, without saying, whether Clare might have followed Nellie Jack John into the ground and they were now both alive hundreds of years ago. Nellie Jack John would be able to deal with it, but Clare never.

Eileen was waiting. 'I couldn't go,' she said. 'I'd not know where.'

'Eileen can't frame in the snow,' said Frank.

'Nor Clare,' said Eileen. 'She's to look after all hours, and turn your back and she's off.'

'You did right, Mother,' said Frank. 'I've to milk, but we'll send these lads off. Now, Eileen, have you a blanket? They can take that and might find it useful.'

The blanket was red and marked 'The Monks' Infirmary' in a silky thread. They had been sold off when the Infirmary closed. Keith had one at home, and the dog used to sleep on it. But for David it might have been on his mother's bed; he looked and was unable to speak about it.

'She can't have gitten so varry far,' said Frank. 'She's so crammly and dindling. But she'd likely be clemmed, and a blanket is best.'

Eileen showed them where the track started.

They went along it. Quite often someone had fallen over. It had not been Nellie Jack John but someone much shorter.

She had cut herself. There were small dark traces of blood. In one place there were some fragments of green glass.

The trail did not go to the Shooting Box. It struck up the hill, round the top of Jingle Beck before that plunged solid down its fall into the Giants' Cradle, and went up towards the moor below the Shooting Box.

Stitching up it went the strides of Nellie Jack John. Haltingly after them were the continual scrapes of Clare.

At the crest of the moor the track changed. From this point Nellie Jack John had gone on alone, and without the sledge. Its track had gone to one side, as if he had pushed it away.

Clare's marks led to where the sledge had been. It was no longer there. Her prints were no longer there.

The sledge had rejoined Nellie Jack John's trail, running on, or to one side or the other, of it.

It had run free, with Clare on it.

140

Down the hillside, like some fatal destination, was only the top of the quarry, with its cliff beyond and below, its fall to the ground at the bottom.

At the edge of the snow lay a crooked pair of spectacles with pink sparkly frames. They looked out over the dale, seeing nothing.

XIX

David looked back the way they had come. At the bottom of the hill Swang Farm was speckled in blue dusk. In its wall the kitchen window glowed. On its roof the thaw-bruised snow was heavy as marzipan.

Leading up from it was the combined track of Nellie Jack John, Clare, and the two boys themselves.

'We fouled that up,' said David. 'We should have walked to one side.'

'Why?' said Keith.

He was not thinking about that, and wondered why David was. They should be facing the other way, seeing what had happened ahead of them. His mind was racing but not going forward; slipping in the slush, digging deeper in.

David's look back had been a brief one. He knew what to do, and was spending a few seconds making sure what they did next was based on what had already really happened.

Keith was approaching the same things from a different angle. When Nellie Jack John had come out of the past he been terrified by the present and plunged down the hill out of the castle. In the morning David and Keith had seen him lying among the trees.

On that hillside Keith had prayed not to find him dead. Now he prayed again, not about finding Clare dead at the foot of the quarry (which he was certain of) but about being able to deal with it.

'We've got to be sure what happened,' said David. 'And whether it did. We've destroyed the evidence, that's all.'

'The more you take, the more you leave behind,' said Keith. 'Footsteps. From a Christmas cracker.'

'So stand still and work it out,' said David, ignoring him. 'Nellie Jack John came up first, followed by Clare. I don't think he knew she was following him. At the top here he pushed the sledge to one side, on that flattish bit so it wouldn't run away alone. Then he went on down to the quarry.'

'He wouldn't have been meaning to fall off,' said Keith. 'We could shout for him.' He drew a special breath, as if it mattered, and cupped his hands. 'Nellie,' he called.

A muted and stuffy echo came dull back. Otherwise there was only the snow slope down to Swang, and ahead but hidden the lights of the town.

'Then,' said David, 'Clare came up. She went to the sledge. And then it ran away with her down the hill the way Nellie Jack John went. So we'll walk to one side of the track and see what happened.'

'If you didn't know about the sledge being by itself,' said Keith, 'you'd think she caught up with him.'

'We obscured everything up to that point,' said David. 'We'd better find her. We'd better find them both.'

It would be best, Keith thought, if some other agency turned up now and took over. A policeman, an ambulance, a choir of angels.

The tracks went through a little valley that brought together the steady plod of Nellie Jack John and the wider glide of the sledge spurs. Twigs of firewood lay like dark cracks. David and Keith walked on the sides of the valley.

Keith's feet slipped. 'It's dragging me in,' he said, spreading his arms, falling back on the slope, making the only angel in the snow with his moving arms.

The lip of snow on the edge of the quarry had been torn, either by Nellie Jack John or by the sledge. There was a gap now, waiting for them.

David picked up the glasses and folded them into his shirt pocket. The rims could not sparkle. The lenses were smeared with darkness.

It was not easy to get to the edge without going over it. Snow dribbled from it, pushed by their hands. The grainy chunks coughed as they landed.

Here the quarry was not immediately vertical, but began with a broken, steep, hillside. The sledge had gone down this steep hill.

Now it was parked beside a block of stone, right way up, tidy on its track. It had no passenger.

'We'll have to go down,' said David. 'To see she didn't fall off on the way. I would have.'

They both slid and rolled. Keith thought it would be snow and might be fun. But heather stems he was holding snared his fingers as his feet lost grip, and before he had recovered from that he found that snow below covered newly broken rock ragged as huge sugar-lumps. Falling down it was like swallowing yourself with your own sore throat.

'We'll never get back up,' said David. 'My leg.' He was now sitting on the sledge rubbing his knee.

'Elbows,' said Keith.

Keith's elbows were restored to him. For some time they had filled the whole sky with pain. Now they were back and working he was able to think of other things, sniffing now, smelling air.

'Blood?' said David. 'Nose?'

'Smoke,' said Keith. 'A fire.' It was wood smoke, still moist, not having carried far.

'He's all right,' said David, catching the smell himself now. 'He'll be down below.'

Beyond this point the quarry face went down in one big sloping step to its clear and level floor. Nothing had touched the snow, approached or left the foot of the cliff, or fallen down.

Clare had lost a mitten on the way. David picked it up, soaked and next to frozen. He took up the rope of the sledge.

Keith shook the red blanket. He folded it again, with snow stuck to it.

The scent of wood smoke grew stronger at a hole in the overhang. There was an ancient geological slip of the rock here, and in the join a dark entry.

'It's a lead mine,' said David.

'Guessing,' said Keith.

'No,' said David. He was in the cleft now and reaching upwards. 'There are wooden beams to hold it up,' he said. 'It's all hillside above.'

The beams were pieces of tree with the bark on, laid as level as possible. Above them stone flags formed a ceiling.

'They're in here,' said Keith. 'With a fire.'

'If we can't see,' said David 'we can sniff along.'

'We can shout,' said Keith. The last time he was underground he carried the candle that created the time-warp for Nellie Jack John; and for David, who had been lost for months, lost for dead, his name on a grave empty of him. But he had been in a cave, and for him only a moment had passed. Keith had brought the candle that unlocked time for him. He had set it back where Nellie Jack John had found it; and together they came back to their own day.

Keith did not know where that cave was. Now he was glad to be without any reminder of candles.

David was shouting now for Nellie Jack John. Before he shouted there was quiet. After he shouted there was a peculiar silence. Then a rustle of tumbling sand above the roof, and continuing darkness.

'No one,' said Keith.

There was a thread of sound from far away, not quite a voice, though it began as one.

Like someone kissing the spout of a watering can, Keith thought, that short reverberation to someone listening inside, the scrapy swirl of water. Then no more kiss.

'A small echo,' said David.

A piece of firewood snapped under Keith's foot.

There was more noise, continuing noise, a high wailing. Keith thought of a lair of wild cats, black, snarling, big enough to eat sheep.

'It's a den,' he said. 'Leopards.'

There was a second voice, using words that could not be made out.

'Neanderthals, said David. 'Giants.' Nellie Jack John's taking of the candle had warped time here and there, and other things had once walked abroad, and might again.

But here was Nellie Jack John again, carrying a light again, but this time knowing where he was and when it was. Once he had been coming out of the ground into a strange world. Now he was like a householder at his own door, expecting his visitors to come in.

'You should have langled her,' he was saying, coming out of the darkness. He meant hobbled her, front leg to back leg. He had been seeking his way through time and the hill. 'She followed on, and this is my only time off, and I's laiting of t'road home, so tek her back and by, wilt'a.'

'We've come for her,' said David. 'We never brought her.'

'You're daft eneuf,' said Nellie Jack John. 'Come by; I can mek nowt of her.' He was shivering and cold in his pullover, without a coat.

The light he carried was an electric torch, not any mysterious candle. He had brought batteries for it once, Keith told him.

'Many a time,' said Nellie Jack John. 'And her, she's that twined at being left alone, harken. I've litten a fire, so let's get back to't and thou can have her.'

XX

'Mind,' said Nellie Jack John, 'thou'll not ken t'road out. Thou'll niver get up yon brant bank and ower t'comb. We'll gan on and out t'other end.'

'Up the bank and around that overhang?' said David. 'No. But we don't know the other end, either.'

'I came thruff ya time,' said Nellie Jack John.

They were in single file in the dark. Only an occasional flash of the torch showed the way at all. 'Thou mun keep ho'd of my coat tail,' said Nellie Jack John, 'ti gan thruff this angle.'

'It's a tight bit,' said David.

The sledge was sometimes being pulled, other times being walked on its end. It was heavy, made very solid fifty years since and meant to last, not designed for narrow ways through the limestone.

All the time someone ahead was crying and calling. Nellie Jack John shouted ahead in no very comforting way, that there was 'no need to baul'.

Then there was light and smoke and a warm place. There was a cave, a widening of the passage.

Clare was sitting on a lumpy rock by a small and flaming fire of kindling. Thin smoke went up to the roof, and was being drawn away.

'He didn't go there,' said Clare. She had not been crying tears, but indignation. 'I saw the lights in the windows. You showed me where it was, Davy. Mams was there. It was our house. So I followed Nellie Jack John because he goes there. But he didn't. I'm glad I don't like him.'

'Nobody was there but the sun,' said Keith. 'We saw it the other day. Nobody was there.'

'I'll git theer,' said Nellie Jack John. 'Then I's off ti Eskeleth. I'll follow t'reek, the way miners do.'

'Follow the smoke,' said David. 'Did they do that?'

'I found Jonty's clay,' said Nellie Jack John, showing them a clay pipe, black inside, shiny outside, cave-wet. 'Jonty would sit in t'mine bottom, and smoke his clay, and t'miners would ken t'road out to air. This is how I'll deea.'

'Die?' said Keith.

'Do,' said David.

'Deea,' said Nellie Jack John.

'Day,' said Clare, joining the nursery game. 'It was Mams's lantern in the window.' But she did not think so now. 'Weren't it?'

David then took the torch from Nellie Jack John and shone it on John's face.

'I thought so,' he said.

'Nowt,' said Nellie Jack John. 'I've had wor blows.'

'This is a worse blow too,' said David. Nellie Jack John's face was covered in blood, and there was a cut on his forehead.

He told them how it happened.

At the shoulder of the moor he had pushed the sledge to one side after taking the bundle of firewood. He thought he could come back up, but hadn't reckoned on so much snow at the top of the quarry. So he had got down and begun to worry. He put his firewood in the entry to the mine, and tried for a long time to climb out.

He was still at it when the sledge came down the same way and landed on him, flattening him and cutting his head. 'Knocked my end in a lile bit,' he said. 'Nowt so mich; not t'boggan, but them hopples.' He meant the braces on Clare's legs.

He had found himself clutching something both soft and bony, and let go of it.

'I thowt it were t'boggart,' he said. 'But it were that,' nodding at Clare, 'nowt ner worse, but I got a fire lit to dry it, whativer.'

'There's a wet mitten,' said David, handing it over. 'Glasses in my pocket.'

'We've to get away out,' said Nellie Jack John.

'We're lost if we go on,' said Keith. 'We should go back and climb down if we can't climb up.'

'We s'll gan on,' said Nellie Jack John. 'Eh? And after, if we don't frame so well we'll gan back and shout and set the moor alight. It's the time of year to burn it.'

'I want Eileen,' said Clare.

'Thou should have kept her when thou had her,' said Nellie Jack John.

Clare shone a red light at him, and then part of a green one. The glass of her torch had broken on the way here. 'I'm cut too,' she said. 'But I won't show you.' She sucked her thumb.

'John, you'll just have to bleed,' said David.

'I will,' said Nellie Jack John. 'We'll get agate. We'll be a lang time, bringing that.' He meant Clare. 'Give us the 'boggan. Hap t'bairn in t'blanket.'

Keith wrapped the blanket like a sling stretcher round her, taking back Nellie Jack John's anorak and putting it on him.

The sling was the best way to bring Clare along. Nellie Jack John turned the sledge on its back and loaded his firewood between its runners. 'It's to carry, whativer,' he said. 'Now we gan on. If we get out of t'reek, then we's off t'road.'

Two ends of the tunnel they were in let air through, but not humans. A third led them into wider ways. 'I don't get lost so easy,' said Nellie Jack John. 'We've been all miners and that. And I ha' my luck-stone on a bit of band, like we all did.'

The wider ways turned into something like rooms. Their voices would echo, and tumbling waters somewhere seemed to say light was near, that the surface was not far away. There was an uphill road now, with Nellie Jack John ahead sniffing and lifting his head. He would now and then show his torch. Now and then, too, Clare shone her green light or her red one.

'T'roof is ower high,' said Nellie Jack John, shining the torch up and showing only a vague reflection from rock. Keith wondered how it mattered, but Nellie Jack John said that the smoke was up there now, not down below, and it was time to make more. 'Grand stuff is matches,' he said. 'And a pinch of a firelighter.'

He lit a fire there and then. It was for smoke, not warmth. These caves were not so cold as the night outside.

'It's not so far,' Nellie Jack John said as they left it and followed its reek. 'We haven't a mile to go.'

Then, some more dark time gone, 'Right,' he said, 'I've been on this road afore. Time to bake clay pie, see-est-a.'

'I want to be out,' said Clare. 'I'm colding.'

Small though she was, David and Keith were glad to set her down in her red blanket sling. But they could not stand still.

'Wait on,' Nellie Jack John told them. 'Smoke walks.'

By rising firelight – and Nellie Jack John was making a bigger fire this time – Keith picked up scattered firewood. The wood was mostly twigs, some broken, some big enough to have been sawn. They were all irregular. But one piece had been made its shape. It was a particular shape too.

'Nellie Jack John,' said Keith, and he felt something urgent in his voice in spite of trying to be calm. 'When you came out of the caves the second time, with David and me, what were you doing?'

'Braying t'drum,' said Nellie Jack John. 'As well as ever I might,

152

thou great fool, for I'd lost yan o' them sticks and had it to do single-handed. What for?'

'I just found a drumstick,' said Keith. 'We've been here before.'

'Then this is t'road,' said Nellie Jack John. 'I's not so far off. You come wi' me, and we'll live at Eskeleth, nay, join the regiment wi' me, I'll set you right; and she, she can bide wi' my sister, or our Kath. Wilt'a?'

'What's he saying?' said Clare. 'It's my house we're going to.'

David was shining the torch about now. His hand shook as he did so. 'How long have we been gone now?' he said. 'Not again, Keith, not again.'

In this cave once there had been another thing. There had been light.

There had been a candle set on a table, and a flame on it.

'Ya time,' said Nellie Jack John, 'I drummed and these fellows waked and I seed t'candle.'

In this place now there was a gathering of tall stone. From some corner of fancy or memory Keith fashioned or recalled a band of horsemen settling back to sleeping rock. Here too was one figure separate, standing but sleeping. The shifting fire and torchlight made it shift too.

'Shadows,' said David. 'Something happened. I don't remember. It all moved. Time. It's how she came back now.' He meant Clare.

A stalactite hung from the roof. Its fellow stalagmite stood below it single and straight, like a candle, on a raised flat rock like a table.

For a moment light flickered on that stone candle.

A drop of water from above, Keith thought. It must be. This is not that time or place again. But time shifted once, and perhaps this is David's sister from another dimension, who will now go back and we shall be rid of her.

'Time has gone wrong again,' said David. 'It is right and wrong, both.'

'It is a candle,' said Clare. 'It is a candle burning. Who lit it? It wasn't there.'

She was out of the blanket now, treading it down, as near kicking it as she could get, and bringing herself along to the stone table.

'I can see into it,' she said. 'It is all burning.'

'Reflection,' said David, turning off the torch.

With the torch off they could still see.

'It is real,' said Clare, reaching out her hand to it. 'This is what we want. I could do anything I want with that light.' But her hand could not get so far, and her legs would not allow her to climb.

It seemed to all three boys that her face was illuminated for a time by something they could not themselves see. And then they were once more in great darkness.

Nellie Jack John kicked the fire into sparks and across the cave. 'We'd best get on,' he said. 'This is not a canny start.'

'No,' said Keith.

'Best be away,' said David.

'Another time,' said Clare. 'Now I know.'

It is already another time, Keith thought. We have gone back to our own again. But she is still here.

They had another fire further on, standing beside it for a while and moving on again. This one too was kicked across the floor, sparking and spluttering with a different smell.

'It's the firelighters,' said Keith.

After a short time they were in a place that sounded different. There was something less solid around them, and David said he half-expected sky to show, and stars.

'I heard a sheep,' said Keith.

'There's wind,' said Nellie Jack John. 'I ken this spot. I took a tumble here once ower, so gan softly.'

Nellie Jack John shone the torch upwards and they saw a made roof with wooden beams, squared and worked, with joists between them and stone flags laid on top, ceiling to this place, and possibly floor to some other.

Nellie Jack John walked against more wood. He shone the torch down. Beside him were man-made shapes too. There were wooden barrels, four of them, crusted over with a shiny dark substance. One barrel was broken.

'That fetched me over,' said Nellie Jack John. 'Upscuttled me another night.'

Keith knew exactly where they were and what these barrels were.

'Billy heard you,' he said. 'You frightened her. We're under the Shooting Box, which was the powderhouse for the lead mines, and these barrels are full of shot powder. High explosive. It's all washed out by wet, but it's still here.'

From the way they had come the smoke was rising in greater clouds, getting into their throats.

Along the edge of a rock a scutter of little sparks was marching, bright and advancing, each one a miniature explosion with dark smoke.

'We'd best be out of this,' said Nellie Jack John. 'If we're under yon spot then that's t'floor. Get it lifted.'

But before they could figure how, the ceiling above began to shift and make noises and thuds, to drop pebbles on them, and scatter fine hard dust; to be opening and snarling.

XXI

There was a run of foggy flame behind them. At the edge of the
flames there was a sharp little report, like a cat spitting.

There was rubble falling from above, and banging and scraping.

'It's shifting in,' said Nellie Jack John. 'We'll ha' to git back.
We'll not git on thruff.'

The way beyond was a narrow gap in the wall of the room. 'I
tummled out of it a bit back,' he said. 'And landed in them barrels.'

The way they had come was now a swirl of smoke, showing in
the light of creeping flames. The floor and part of the walls had been
set alight.

Gravelly stuff fell from above, and the noise of more to come.
David was up on a barrel, trying to hold the stone back with his
hands.

'I saw light,' he said. 'Another fire up here.'

Keith was holding the blanket over Clare's head, and holding her
up too. She was coughing, which caused her pain, and made her
fearful of what went on around her. New appearances of flames did
not alarm her, because they meant nothing, but she was looking at
Nellie Jack John, David, and Keith, and saw they did not know
what to do.

David was looking down, to keep dust from his eyes. Keith saw
his expression change from one of worry to one of terror. David
screamed.

Keith dropped Clare. Nellie Jack John came away from his

vain burrowing. They both went to David, who was fighting something above him, out of sight in the cascade of rubbish, fighting and shouting, being drawn upwards, his feet leaving the ground.

Fragments were falling down; smoke was going up; there was a huge amount of shouting, and the spiteful chatter of small explosions in the fire.

Then David won free. He dropped down again, bent over and clutching his wrists.

'There's something there,' he said. 'Biting. It grabbed me.'

There was a moment without words. It ended with a crashing blow overhead, more falling sand, and light shining down. Frank Watson was shouting at them, his head in an opening overhead, where he had lifted first one flag and then another of the floor of the Shooting Box.

He had taken David's wrists and tried to pull him out of the cellar of that building.

'Thoo lile beggar,' he said, loudly. 'What are you doing in there? Come away out. By, I thought it were t'boggart. Who's there? Come away out and look sharp.'

They handed Clare up first. A corner of the red blanket was burning. David was next, standing there already. Keith and Nellie Jack John could almost climb out alone.

They were in the larger room of the Shooting Box. In its floor was the hole where Frank had lifted flags to bring all four of them through.

'I came for this stuff,' said Nellie Jack John, jumping easily down the hole again and handing up the sledge. 'So it's right in the end.'

'Get away out,' said Frank. 'Don't be so daft.'

There was a suitcase in the room, and beside it a wicker basket. Nellie Jack John set them on the sledge, and pulled the sledge out of the door.

'Don't stop,' said Frank. 'That's gunpowder burning in there. We'll be off.'

He had come up on the Land-Rover. Sledge, case, basket, Nellie Jack John, Keith, went in the back. David was in front holding Clare. The Land-Rover rolled down the hill before the engine started. Then Frank was sliding it down between banks of snow.

'It'll go,' he said, looking back towards the Shooting Box. 'I always said. It'll go like a bomb.'

'But what are you going to do?' asked David.

'Nowt,' said Frank. 'We've to get that lile lass back to Eileen first of all. She's tewing herself sick at losing what isn't hers worse than if it were. Then we'll see.'

Eileen was waiting for them in the yard. She was casting an eye up the hill towards the Shooting Box. She was angry at not knowing what was going on.

'Smoke,' she said 'We saw smoke, and Frank went to look for you, Keith, and all the time you were setting a fire.'

'No,' said David.

'As for you, Nellie Jack John, John Cherry of Eskeleth,' Eileen went on, 'there's not so much more I'll want from you, my lad. You did neither right nor fittingly, and I don't know that I want you here at all.'

'No,' said Keith, wanting to explain.

'And as for you, David, 'doctor or not, your father kept all his sense to himself when he fathered you. I say begone.'

'No, Mother,' said Nellie Jack John.

'And you, miss, I should send you out in the snow again. I don't know where you belong, but I've no call to keep you, and I'm not bound to.'

'Mother,' said Frank.

'Oh Frank', said Eileen, putting her hands to her face, 'he called me Mother. Oh, John Cherry, is that right for you?'

'Happen,' said Nellie Jack John, looking away and at the Land-Rover.

'And I wasn't being nice to you,' said Eileen. 'Do you mean it?'

'You meant it,' said Nellie Jack John, looking straight at Eileen. 'So that meks me mean it. Noo, I's clemmed, so put t'kettle on. And thou,' he went on to Clare, because he had to take his eyes away from Eileen, 'thou come thy ways.'

He picked her up, carried her a few paces towards the house, then handed her to David. 'Family,' he said. She was very tense at being carried.

At the house Eileen took her away. 'Don't be so heavy,' she told her. 'You next,' she said to Nellie Jack John. 'I can't have you with a broken head like that.'

'I'll get milking,' said Nellie Jack John.

'Aye,' said Frank. 'Best frame like we mean to.' He put his hand on Nellie Jack John's shoulder for a moment, and they went off together to the shippon.

The yard was silent. Up on the hill flames danced in still air, making no sound, showing nothing but themselves. Sparks flew up like slow tracer. There was perhaps a smell of cinders.

'The roof has fallen in,' said Keith. 'That'll be it. There's no more to burn. My dad looks after that place.'

'You'll get the blame,' said David. 'It belongs to Lord Zig-Zag. Dad calls him that.'

Eileen told them from the bathroom window to go in and put the kettle on. She went back to shrieking at Clare in a fierce but friendly way.

'She's got a family,' said Keith.

The Shooting Box had not finished. It now blew up. There was a punchy but muffled bang, in the ground as well as in the air. There was the gruff sound of settling and falling stone; for a moment there was a fountain of sparks and flame lighting a higher rising puff or plume of smoke. Then that blinked out and the hillside was empty.

David put the kettle on the stove. He saw Keith standing filthy in the light. He looked at his own hands.

'You're wearing your ugly idiot clothes,' he said. 'And your ugly idiot skin.'

Keith thought David was the same, daubed with cave mud, wet with snow, grimed completely with ash. The right return insult escaped his mind. There was hot water at the sink, and they washed. Keith felt like falling asleep under the hot water.

'He won't get back in there,' said David. 'Nellie Jack John won't. He won't ever get back home. I mean, we knew he hadn't, but now we know he can't.'

'They've turned time off,' said Keith, remembering the stone candle.

Eileen came down then, drying her hands on a pink towel. 'I don't like to do this,' she said. 'Maybe you'd do it better. The bedroom's that cold.'

She wanted a shovel of fire taken upstairs. It was the right time to carry red embers with no smoke coming from them. David carried the coal bucket after Keith and tipped it on the grate. Smoke went green up the chimney.

Keith went to Nellie Jack John's room and laid a dark drumstick on the chest by the window. Beside the chest stood the drum and the other drumstick. Nellie Jack John said it belonged to the regiment, and would not let it go to a museum.

In the bed, hardly showing, Clare's glasses glimmered at them, like the jewel of lead. She was asleep behind them when they looked. David lifted them from her face.

XXII

Clare was in the garden at Swang, through the wall beyond the orchard, Eileen said, busy with something, but watching for any activity and planning to join it.

'Like a little cat,' said Eileen. 'Follows and follows. If I wait for her she takes a hig; if I don't she gets twined with herself. But wants to be in everything that's going off.'

'More like a lile cur,' said Nellie Jack John. 'Wants chaining up.'

'No,' said Eileen. 'She's all Miss Independence, and I won't change that.'

'A house dog,' said Nellie Jack John, and used his word for contemptible rubbish, 'ket'. He went off with the real dog to see about lambs.

'No,' said Eileen, to the closed door. 'She's not a dog. She doesn't think she's a human. Well, of course she does because she is, but she doesn't want to be anyone else.'

It was now summer, close on Whitsuntide. David and Keith had come up to see Nellie Jack John about going to the fair on Monday in the market place.

'I thought we wouldn't tell her,' said Keith.

'She wouldn't like it,' said David. 'She could only get on baby rides. All that independence.'

'Doesn't know what she should like,' said Keith.

'That wouldn't suit,' said Eileen. 'Nothing suitable will. Not school, for one.'

163

They all knew about school. Eileen and Billy had gone with Clare when she looked at it. Clare had decided it would not do, Eileen reported. 'It's a special school,' Clare had said. 'They are for other people.' She wanted a school that had only the usual sort of pupil.

The taxi had come one morning and driven her there. She had done as she did with Eileen, and taken a hig. She had been very angry.

'So would I be,' David had said. 'She just wants to get on with real stuff.'

Keith thought that people should use what is provided, if it was right for them.

'A right wick-belly-wengis,' Nellie Jack John said.

Clare had walked out and gone along the road to an ordinary school. That school had sent her back to the special school. She had fallen down in one of her states and been returned to Swang.

She would not get into the taxi again. It stopped coming. The authorities wondered what to do.

'She gets bad in the night if she's crossed, and that's it,' said Eileen. 'You can't even take her hand. Doesn't like a fuss, she says. Calls out for Boggy, and he comes. Won't thank you for anything out of the way. Tell her she's good, or brave, or owt, and she would brain you.'

David might be able to do something, Eileen said. 'She's got eyes only for you,' she told him.

'She thinks David is her brother,' said Keith.

'It's a lovely fancy,' said Eileen.

But now Clare only said that David could teach her better than school. 'Nellie Jack John doesn't know so much,' she told him. 'And Keith hates me.'

I don't hate her, Keith thought. She isn't a good idea, that's all.

164

Everything is untrue. But he could not do as David demanded, and prove it.

Last year school time had been wasted by investigations into fights with soldiers and lads from away. This year the school was to be self-witnessing and uninvolved.

Dr Tate had divided the school into groups, given them interests at the fair, and wanted a full report by Wednesday. 'Monitor yourselves,' he said. 'Remember last year. This year it's the science of human behaviour.' He eyed Year 8. 'More or less.'

Nellie Jack John found his way down without saying anything to Clare. 'She hears owt,' he said. 'But I've gitten away and I'll try plenty of rides and all the stalls. I might get in mischief.' He meant a sharp fight with bare fists. 'For all your speiring.'

The year before he had been completely dazzled by colour and sound and the electric movement of rides and booths, and had wandered round gaumless, he had said, 'Mekking nowt on't. Yonderly.'

This year he felt he had the sense of it. At once he won a large yellow rabbit on a quoits game.

'6.17 p.m. John Cherry has won a yellow rabbit,' David wrote. 'To be named Buck, after its father.'

Keith was getting the life history of the stall-holder.

'By Gow,' Nellie Jack John was saying, 'I'll have one more turn, the last time of all. I might get the best of it.'

He did not mean the quoits game. He meant another attempt to win Billy's favour. He went off to the Dodgems. At first he was wanting to walk about on the floor of the ride, finding it made his hair stand on end. He was taken away from there. He and the yellow rabbit had a car to themselves.

'You drive,' said David to Keith, keeping Nellie Jack John under observation.

165

'Three for ten pence,' the quoits stall-holder was saying to Keith. 'You can win every time, every time. That's two hundred per cent likely. That's value for money.'

Nellie Jack John was riding in a manner of his own. He was not circulating but driving for collisions. Some of them were accidental, but there was one other car he aimed for time after time.

Billy, in that other car, was waving him away, and he was taking no notice. In the end he got out of his car, leaving it stranded, and went to sit on Billy's.

He was taken away from there by a biggish attendant. Nellie Jack John wanted to fight. The yellow rabbit was run over and broke one of the cars. Two attendants took Nellie Jack John away and warned him off.

'Nay, it's right,' he was saying when David caught up with him. 'She won't wait of me. I've tried my last time. I can look annywheer else, never no matter.'

At the Dodgems, Keith was helping Billy from her car, and having an arm ready for Clare. Billy pulled her out.

'I thought you would bring her,' said Billy. 'But I went on for her anyway.'

'We're working,' said Keith, waving his notebook, feeling guilty and thinking he deserved to.

'You didn't want me,' said Clare.

'Of course not,' said Billy. 'Same as I don't want Nellie Jack John, but he doesn't understand. I'm not waiting for him, or anyone. It isn't what happens.'

'He's very old-fashioned,' said Keith.

'Thinks he's just got to say and I'll wait,' said Billy. 'That doesn't happen any more. Where was he brought up?'

'One fatality,' David wrote in his book. 'Large yellow rabbit, affectionately known as Buck. Next of kin sulking.'

'One broken heart,' said Keith, reading it. 'Not affectionately known at all.'

Nellie Jack John was now busy not winning a goldfish too.

'That's not science,' said David. 'That's natural history.'

Keith was at the Shooting Box later in the month. His father was taking notes.

'Looks as if something fell *into* it,' said Mr Heseltine. 'Not as if it exploded upwards.'

'Whooshed,' said Keith. 'As if a firework got soggy but still worked.'

There was a gap in the middle of the roof. The ridge had then sagged from either end, as if the hole that connected them had had weight and pulled them down. The beams and joists were black, and wet with weather.

The door had been scorched open and was now jammed on its stone sill.

'We'll just go carefully,' said Mr Heseltine, wrenching it back against the wall.

Inside there was a crater where the stone-flagged floor had been, the flags tumbled down into it broken, washed clean by rain. Large beams that had held them were tipped and charred and eaten by fire.

'You can see the wall of a cellar,' said Mr Heseltine. 'The building lay unused a hundred years. There was a tale about gunpowder all that time, but nothing to be seen because we didn't know there was a cellar and didn't look. But that doesn't mean gunpowder. People just like that sort of story. Then it was a shooting box; but there isn't any shooting down here now.'

'The story was right,' said Keith. 'Gunpowder. All the flames shot up suddenly.'

'Unlikely,' said his father. 'You saw the roof fall in. If it wasn't for Frank Watson coming up here and hearing you, and seeing you, no one would believe what you two said.'

'We wouldn't have been there to say,' said Keith. 'Not that we ever get believed. Like last time.'

'I believe, Keith,' said Mr Heseltine. 'So don't look so hurt. In the end I had to believe what happened that other time too. But there are plenty of people who can't take in an unfamiliar fact, even if they are there. So I shall tell his Lordship that it burnt out from an unknown cause, and that I've sent in the bulldozer and made it safe.'

'Lord Zig-Zag,' said Keith, and his father laughed.

'Nellie Jack John will want to go down under there,' said Keith. 'Looking for a way out. We were nearly there.'

'That's one of those unfamiliar facts,' said his father, 'which doesn't get believed in. So I shan't remind the owner. Nellie Jack John can put up with being here. I hear he's getting used to Eileen. Calls her Mother, doesn't he?'

'Only if he's cross,' said Keith.

'He's got nothing to be cross about,' said Mr Heseltine. 'He should just be grateful.'

Keith said nothing. He knew that agreement would be easier than working matters out. He did something easier, working on what David's response to his father's remark would be.

He saw a shred of evidence of something, stranded on a ledge in the cellar wall, where he had put it.

He scrambled down for it, the clay pipe Nellie Jack John had found in the cave. But it could prove nothing to anyone else. He was clear then about what David would have said. David would not allow Nellie Jack John the burden of being grateful. Nellie Jack John had a right to care, and to be free, and others had a duty to provide that care and freedom and need not be thanked.

'Thinking?' said Mr Heseltine.

'Yes,' said Keith, wondering what he would have to forget if he became a solicitor.

Three days later the Shooting Box was a mound of rubble. No one would squat there now.

The next evening Keith was at David's house. They were eating soup that Sister Mackenzie had made.

'He keeps making speeches,' said David, talking about a play they were reading at school. 'It's not conversation. People don't do that.'

'You never met my dad, or something?' said Keith.

The telephone rang. Sister Mackenzie was there to answer it. 'He's here,' she said. 'David.'

'Yes,' said David, into it.

'Away,' said the voice at the other end. And that was all. The line was cut off.

'Very laconic,' said Sister Mackenzie. Everyone had heard the message.

'Doesn't like the telephone,' said David.

'We'd better go,' said Keith. They both knew who it was. Sister Mackenzie watched calmly, smiling gently. Supposing it was some childish game, Keith thought. He did not know what it was, but the order had to be obeyed.

They left their soup. 'An emergency,' said David. 'You'll be used to them, Sister.'

'Now he can use the telephone,' said David, pedalling hard up the hill towards Swang, 'he could take a mobile with him underground and when he gets to the other end and his own time he can telephone and tell us all about it.'

'If he remembers us in his future,' said Keith.

'Past,' said David.

Nellie Jack John was in the yard of the farm. He looked at them, and up towards the Shooting Box.

'She saw,' he said. 'And she got ken of it from that Billy. I've forgotten her. She bit me.' The back of his hand was torn. 'If it's not ya thing it's anither.'

'What'll we do?' said Keith. Something had to be done, but had no idea what.

'It's thy fault,' said Nellie Jack John. 'Thou and thy dad both, sending to bray the walls down. I niver sent for thee.'

Eileen came into the yard, drying her hands. She was flustered and angry. 'Sometimes he just knows one word,' she said, nodding at Nellie Jack John. 'There's the mother come to fetch her and she won't stir. We can do nowt with her. I don't know, David, whether you can't.'

'Bound to do summat,' said Nellie Jack John.

Billy was sitting on the bottom step of the stairs. She was looking extremely stubborn, as if she had all her arguments ready and flexible, with only one conclusion.

'I've got a room,' she said. 'I came for her. She knows all about that. I never forgot her. I wouldn't do that.'

But Clare wanted some other answer, and to be told it by some other person.

She was in the dry and unused porch inside the front door. She was shaking with misery, and held herself up with the curtain that hung over the outer door. There were no tears, but she was crying.

Her mother was nothing to her; Eileen was nothing to her. She turned her head to look at each of them in turn, and turned it away sharply again. Then she looked at David.

She's going to get her own way, Keith thought. But you can't paddle her, even if a smack would be right. It's a stationary tantrum. But it's about something.

'Now Clare,' said David. 'You'll have to tell me what it all is, because that's what sisters do, and it's what brothers are for. And I'm your brother.'

XXIII

'That was our house,' said Clare. 'That was the only house we ever had. What for did they do that?'

'They give us another spot,' said Billy. 'A room. We've had rooms before.'

Clare clamped her lips together. She was not allowing her chin to wobble her into tears. She shook her head, meaning that David should close the inner door. He put it so that Billy at the foot of the stairs was hidden, but did not quite close it.

What they said Keith could hear; he could see Clare against the curtain.

'My mum could deal with her,' said Billy. 'Rattray couldn't stand it, so he was off.'

'But it got burnt,' David was saying. 'You were in it.'

'You are telling a fib,' she said.

'When we were under the ground,' said David. 'It was dark.'

'You-a are telling-a a fi-ib-a, Davy-a,' she shouted, in a strange emphatic way.

'Right cross,' said Billy. 'Goes on for days. And then some . . .'

'The time you followed Nellie Jack John into a lead mine,' said David. 'I'm not telling a fib. You've forgotten. I wouldn't tell my sister a fib.'

'That was at night,' said Clare, because that was what she remembered. She went on, reasonably, 'We had fires. I was going to sleep in a tree. I can climb trees. You have forgotten, Davy.'

'The roof fell in,' said David. 'You weren't wearing your glasses.'

'I don't need them,' Clare explained. 'The sky broke.' These brothers are such fools, she meant. 'There was a forest fire. It was a forest.'

'We came back in the Land-Rover,' said David.

'Of course, stupid,' said Clare. 'Cars don't go in caves. It was a trip. You forgot to bring the tea.'

'And we didn't eat the mushrooms in case they were toadstools,' said David.

'There was a candle,' said Clare. 'I wanted to stay, but you wouldn't. I could see inside.'

'Some candles are poisonous too,' said David.

'But they shouldn't knock it down,' said Clare, giving in all at once. 'Just because I was made like this.'

'My sister would be sorry she said I told a fib,' said David.

'I expect she is,' said Clare. 'So I'm going to stop here and look after you. That's what happened in the candle and it was better.'

'I saw it once,' said David. 'The candle.'

'I was better,' said Clare. 'I understood it. No more hospical.'

'So did I,' said David. 'No one else does.'

'Keith,' said Clare, mentioning a person who typically wouldn't.

'Old Keith,' said David, trying not to agree or disagree. 'The ugly idiot.'

'I should come to your house,' said Clare. She thought she had won her way, and was now dismissing any tiny options that existed. 'But I don't know the people.'

'Billy will have some nice people,' said David.

'Billy,' said Clare. 'That's not her real name, Davy. Billy was a boy who had the overall last. I should still stay here.'

'She's your mother,' said David.

'No, Davy,' said Clare. 'If she was my mother she'd be your mother too. So that's proved.'

Keith was thinking Dr Tate would call that a good knock-down argument. David was not sure how to answer it. 'But she came for you,' he said.

Clare seemed to think that was a good knock-down argument too, and that the matter was not quite settled. She was working it out.

'She's very sensible,' said Eileen.

'You should go with her,' David was saying to Clare.

'Yes,' said Clare. 'I'll get some work. They have to give it to you. I'll stamp about.' She tried, but could not do that.

David opened the door wider. He looked at Billy, still on the bottom step. She was shaking her head. She wanted Clare to stay here.

'Better,' she said, meaning that out aloud, but not knowing how to express details and difficulties except with an anxious and agile frown.

'Mams,' said Clare, agreeing, but at cross purposes. 'Is it really nice?'

'It's horrible,' said Billy. 'But that ghost monster knocked down our nice house here. I saw as I came along. The new one's up a nasty lift. Neighbours.'

'You should have said,' said Clare.

Eileen was shaking her head. 'But what you all want.' she said, 'and I do too . . .'

'But I'm your brother,' said David, 'and you'd better stay here.'

' . . . is something different,' Eileen finished. 'And I'm doing my best.'

This is all nonsense, Keith was thinking. Good knock-down nonsense, but nonsense. But right.

'It won't be for long,' said Billy.

'It's for now,' said Clare 'Davy.'

She was calling to him in a fading voice. He did not know why.

173

She saw her hands let go of the curtain, though she did not want them to. Then she fell, in one piece to the stone floor, and lay without movement.

'She's killed,' said Keith, because she had fallen heavy as a tree and lay as still as one.

'And then,' said Billy, getting up but not in any hurry. 'They once took her away because of the bruises, but she got that mad at them she did it again and they knew.'

'She does that,' said Eileen. 'Not just when she means to.'

David was picking up her glasses. Billy was picking Clare up awkwardly, but Eileen gathered her up and carried her off. Billy followed.

David thought it was time to go home. Outside it was still early evening. Well-grown lambs were healthily racing about the higher fields, their mothers shouting at them. In the yard Frank was beating a piece of tractor into shape.

'Is it gone?' he said.

'Stopping,' said Keith.

'Not a lot of bother,' said Frank. 'She likes it.'

At the house, bath water ran out of the drain.

'Still here then,' said Nellie Jack John. 'All maks and mannders end up here.'

'All makes and manners,' David translated.

He and Keith rode along the track, one in either rut, aiming in the wet places to spray water over each other.

'Missed me,' said Keith. 'You didn't mean it, did you? Brother and sister.'

'I was telling a lie,' said David, hurrying towards a splash ahead of them. 'But not the one she thought. She might be. You have to look at the possibilities, Keith.'

'Impossibilities, you mean,' said Keith, twisting his handlebars and spattering himself with mud.

'Saying it was twins,' said David. 'It could have been. Both of what we know might be true. What then?'

'You still don't know,' said Keith. 'You still want to believe it if you can.'

'It's possible,' said David, thinking about things and riding straight through a wide puddle that could have drowned Keith, applied in the right way, and almost did.

'You'll know one day,' said Keith, spitting out puddle.

'Today I was just sorting it out,' said David. 'But you should have done it. You're the teaching one. You understand children. Or you wanted to once.'

'I'm not responsible,' said Keith. 'Never was.'

'And I wasn't until I told the lie,' said David. 'But now I am. I've tied it round my neck.'

Then Keith managed to hurl the last dub of water across him and the conversation ended in a drenched draw.

'Eileen Watson telephoned,' said Sister Mackenzie one Saturday.

'Problems?' said Dr Wix. 'That's a sickly child.'

'For David,' said Sister Mackenzie. 'But the same child. You'd understand, she said, about taking some toy there next time. It's being asked for.'

'Muz,' said Keith.

'Muz?' said Dr Wix. 'How could Muz interest her?'

'She's seen him,' said David. 'But he's safe in his box. What's she sickly with?'

'It'll be some long Latin name,' said Dr Wix. 'Not infectious.' He was not about to say.

'You'd be the last to hear about the patients,' said Sister Mackenzie. 'Isn't that so, Ricky?'

A dry week and another dry week, and then a parched month,

followed the droughty winter. Frank looked at his hayfields and saw no growth in them.

'I'm still feeding hay,' he said. 'The lambs should be filling with grass. They'll not fatten and they won't grade for the lamb sales. And there's nowt for cows.'

Nellie Jack John thought that Frank had more cows here under one roof, or in field together, than there had been in the whole of Eskeleth.

Spiders and dust were the only measurable things in the school rain-gauges.

Clare was queen of her summer, she said. She had never sat in a garden, Now she was day in and day out under Eileen's washing-line inside the walls of that garden.

'Not many flowers,' she said. 'Just long grass.'

Frank's idea of gardening was to put some sheep in now and then and keep the grass down. 'Farmers don't make gardeners,' he said.

Eileen pushed the mower about, gathering away stones. Nellie Jack John ran the cooling water-hose from the dairy and damped the garden down.

'I don't like to spend her money,' said Eileen. 'But it's mounting up. The mother brought some more that time. She knew Clare would end up here.'

Eileen used it to buy four garden chairs and a table. Frank moved the washing-line out of the way to the orchard.

'Makes no difference except to the one who has to do it,' he said.

Keith attended a primary school jumble sale. He exchanged a bottle of aftershave from the tombola for four boxes of plants. David had grown dozens of pansies for the Health Centre, and brought the surplus. There were bags of little white daffodils, and tulips the council removed from a roundabout.

Clare would crawl about putting them into the soil, waiting for them to flower at once.

'Next year,' said Eileen. 'You'll see them then.'

Earlier a little almond tree had filled the space within the walls with the flavours of ice-cream.

Now, in the evening, some small scattering of seeds had produced the smell of dolly mixtures.

In the evenings Clare would play cards. Nellie Jack John thought cards were sinful and would have nothing to do with them.

'Thou'lt go in the hull,' he said. 'Like sheep.'

'She can play,' said Eileen. 'She can beat me at anything.'

'We don't know how,' said Keith. 'We've put flowers in. That's it. We've never played cards.'

'You don't know the names of them,' said David.

'Snap,' said Keith.

'You probably think they are clovers,' said David.

Clare more than once asked about Muz.

'He's resting,' said David. Later he told Keith that Muz was to stay in the box.

'But she had him longer than you,' said Keith. 'There's a law about that. Possession is nine points of the mouse.'

'He's mine,' said David. 'It would dishonour you if I beat you up for having him and then gave him away. That's the biggest tenth point of the law. Actually of course there might be a hundred points, so she hasn't most of them. Besides, I possess him now, so they're all mine.'

But Muz sat in his mind. 'If she was my sister she'd have broken him up by now,' he said. 'She never did. Whoever she is. She can have him one day.'

'One day,' he told Clare.

'For ever,' she said. They were playing Casino. She swept up two of his aces and the ten of diamonds and won the game before the hand was complete.

But in the next hand she frightened them both. She began playing wildly, throwing down cards that should have scored for her, and doing nothing sensible; then she dropped the pack she was dealing from, called out in pain, and fell down among the flowers with her eyes shut.

'A long Greek name,' Dr Wix told David next morning. 'We'll have to consider getting her into hospital, Kirstie,' he said to Sister Mackenzie.

XXIV

Keith was working out a way of unfastening Clare from the story of her life that she believed. He was getting the wrong answers, at breakfast.

'You just have to assume some things you can't prove to yourself,' said his father. 'For instance, what are you?'

'Human,' said Keith. 'Male.'

'Describe it,' said Mr Heseltine. 'Human, not male. There are ladies present.'

'Two legs,' said Keith.

'Clothes-peg,' said Mr Heseltine.

'Hairless,' said Keith.

'Slug,' said Mr Heseltine.

'Talking,' said Keith.

'Parrot,' said Mr Heseltine. 'But you assume you are human, and no one will succeed in proving that you aren't. So we have to put up with that. But who are you?'

'But you know who I am,' said Keith.

'Why do you say that?' asked Mr Heseltine.

'Because you told me,' said Keith. 'So I know you know. You gave me my name.'

'Right,' said Mr Heseltine. 'Now prove it to that woman over there.'

'Who is that boy?' said his mother. 'Why is he eating our toast?'

'To tell you the truth, Dolly,' said Mr Heseltine, 'I found him in a Gladstone bag at King's Cross Station one day. I've never been to Victoria. I forget his proper name; but now, Keith, do you still know who you are?'

'Actually, I do,' said Keith. 'I've seen my birth certificate, and that doesn't prove anything. But I have to be someone, and it must be me.'

'Unless it's proved otherwise,' said Mr Heseltine.

David said the same thing later on about Clare.

'I've tried to disprove it,' he said. 'But if it's true in the slightest it's true right through.'

'You went and told her she was right,' said Keith. 'Now you can't ever prove she isn't.'

'It would be easier not having to bother,' said David. 'But I have to.'

'I can't understand why,' said Keith. 'She can't do anything. She isn't anything. We rescued her in the snow. We rescued her in the cave. We keep rescuing her. We've done enough. I am thinking what I want to think, not what anyone else wants.'

'You rescued me in the cave once,' said David. 'You're so sentimental you think you would rescue anyone.'

'It was a long time ago,' said Keith. It had been the year before last, when Keith had brought David back from the edge of the time-warp. 'It was the only logical thing. She hates me.'

'Of course,' said David. 'Look at this.' He brought out a letter and handed it to Keith.

'You could start reading them yourself,' said Keith. 'It's all quite long ago now.'

'It's yesterday,' said David. 'I've read it.'

'Dear Davy,' the letter ran. It was headed from Swang Farm, Frank's rubber stamp on a page of his cash book. There was a blue stain of carbon paper down its back.

★ ★ ★

180

Dear Davy, the spidery and precise hand wrote, *I hope you are well. today I am sic are you Well I hope you are not. But apart from tebe I am well. you have not came to se me, you said, you would. Mtrrht the Pig is going to hav pupies and I am going to kepe 1. Plese com and se me and mrs watsen. Nelie told me abowt the Pig pupies I am lookin fowrad to seing you. I am in bed a lott, your loeing sistre Clare. I am mising you.*

'Just because it's written down,' said Keith, 'doesn't make it important. I never wrote to you. But I never missed you.'

That was not true, of course, but some things are best denied before they appear. David, for instance, thought he was beyond feeling for his mother. He found it less painful to miss his sister; and painful again to find her in this uncertain way.

'Tebe?' said David. 'Tebe?'

'T, E, D, E,' said Keith. 'Letter's the wrong way round. "Tired".'

'I want her to get it right,' said David. 'You could teach her. Or am I being soppy?'

'She's not who you want to think she is,' said Keith. 'So we won't go. We've done it all.'

'I have to,' said David. 'Technically it's my job, even if it isn't logically. There's this too.'

He handed Keith another piece of paper. On one side it said 'Christmas Greetings', in print, and a written message, 'From Tim, Rosie, and the Boys'. Keith turned it over. Here it said,

Excuse paper, David, she is pining away for you to come you know what she thinks of you if its not to much bother, Eileen Watson come any time P.S. your father wants her to go to hosp right soon not for long—

Keith looked up from the words.

'Nobody ever gave you a pig puppy,' said David.

'With you around who needs one?' said Keith. 'We'll have to go. I don't mind.'

That's what she is, he thought, a pig puppy.

Nellie Jack John was in the yard at Swang, busy with some farm business.

'She's not in t'house,' he said. 'She's in that lile garden. Tell her I'll come next. Tell her, next.'

Keith did not know what he meant by next. As soon as possible, perhaps. David did not know.

Clare was sitting in a cardboard box against a pillow of straw, on a bed of it. She was too busy to look up.

'I've got them here,' she said. 'One, two, three, four, five, six, seven pig puppies.'

She was in a nest with newborn black and white piglets. They were milling about trying to find something to hold on to. The litter was not yet complete. Nellie Jack John came next, as he promised, the next being the eighth piglet.

'They git underfoot,' he says. 'And she overlays them, does Martha. There'll be two or three more and then we'll put them back. They're laiting of their mother now.'

'I could feed them,' said Clare. 'If I had two rows of nibbles like Martha.

'Thou'll mek a farmer yet,' said Nellie Jack John, going back to Martha for the next again.

After the next piglet things began to disarrange. Clare leaned back on a corner of the box, which gave way. The piglets at once boiled over and out and began to run about the garden. Clare lay in a heap of straw, unable to get up.

Keith ran about cornering piglets, but the litter was what Dr Tate called an elastic medium, and if he put pressure on them to stay in one place then they boiled over in another like super-cooled helium. Muz would turn away from the edge of a table. Piglets would turn away at any time; the whole world, or the garden, was an edge to them.

Clare was at an eye-level with them, watching, and then not watching, but laying her head down.

David wanted to chase pigs, but Clare made him sit beside her. She was an ugly sight. The baby pigs had trampled on their umbilical cords and trodden a sort of eiderdown-coloured mincemeat over her. Her hands were grimed and stained. Her face was no better.

Pigs escaped into the orchard. Eileen came to see what was happening.

'Time it was over,' she said. 'Now what a mess you've got in, Clare.'

'It's the puppies,' Clare muttered. 'It's the puppies. I can't breathe.'

'Can you do nothing, David?' said Eileen. 'Sit her up again.'

David did not want to touch her. She did not want to be touched.

'Pigs first,' said Eileen.

'I'll keep the one with the black back,' said Clare. 'I'll have to last longer for that. This little piggy.'

'I'd better sit you up,' said David. 'Would you last longer like that?'

'Oh Davy,' said Clare. 'I just want to be here, in the pig-sky.'

He pulled her to the wall and sat her up in the sunshine. She was tense and unthankful. He brought her a pig. 'All these silly legs,' she said, kissing it.

Eileen jammed the cardboard box against two chairs and filled it with pigs. 'Now Miss,' she said to Clare, stealing her pig, picking Clare up. Clare stiffened, and then relaxed.

Nellie Jack John said the sow had finished farrowing, he thought.

They carried the piglets back to her and closed the door on them.

'She wants the one with the black back,' said David.

'It'll have to live out wi' the rest,' said Nellie Jack John.

Inside the house Eileen was setting out some tea. Upstairs it sounded as if Clare might be skipping.

'No,' said Eileen. 'It's him, you know, him.'

'The b . . .' said David.

' . . . oggart,' said Keith. 'I shouldn't have said.'

'She thinks it's a cat or a fox, said Eileen. 'Until now, and it's a pig. It goes along with her. They'll be asleep in a bit. She's only up an hour or so a day. I'd bring her a bed down here, but no, she thinks she might look ill. She still says things out of nature, that one, waiting to be born her own self, she thinks. Says she knows it all, but she won't tell Frank the score draws for Saturday.'

She had written to David. A week later she telephoned him. Sister Mackenzie rang the call through from the Health Centre to the house. 'You can speak now, caller,' she said. 'He is on the line.'

'Hello,' said David. 'We've got a lot of work today. A lot.' But in a little while he was saying yes all the time, and then he was speaking to Eileen.

'We'd better go up,' he said when he had put the telephone down. 'They're coming to take her to hospital.' The ambulance would be along to Swang about three o'clock, Eileen said, and some of the bairn's things were packed. No pigs, though.

'Why is she going in?' said Keith. He knew perfectly well the general effect of going into a hospital, but needed more detail.

'It won't make any difference,' said David. 'We still have to go to Swang.'

Sister Mackenzie said only that certain things could not be done at the patient's home, and weel, Keith, maybe some things could never be done at all, so we should leave it at that. We can do no more.

They still had to go to Swang.

Clare was lying on her bed. She was fully clothed but not ready to go anywhere. The sockets of her eyes were blue, like bruises. Eileen said it was pain, not weeping.

'I shall stick down,' said Clare. 'They won't be able to get me up.'

'We can visit you,' said David. 'They have special times for kids.'

'Just until you grow up,' said Clare. 'Don't tell Mams. She doesn't like it when I come out, because hospical always makes me ill. They cut my hair. I don't want to go. I haven't time. I always take Muz. I want Muz. Where is Boggy? Who will look after the pigs?'

The ambulance sent shimmers of light into the room, its white paint papering the walls with it.

'Who's going to look after you, Davy?' said Clare.

'I'll just take her bag down,' said Eileen. 'We shall miss you, Clare. Just come back soon.'

Keith picked up the bag and handed it to Eileen. As soon as she took it the two little locks sprang open. The clothes inside leapt out, not falling, but rising into the air, tangling and twirling, and going like a whirlwind through the room.

'Now,' said Eileen, 'stop that. They're all just to put back.'

'Boggy,' said Clare. 'A good fox.'

The good fox had not finished. Eileen was picking up the scatter of clothes, and getting cross, she said. Miss, she said.

Clare chuckled.

Outside the ambulance turned itself about. The back doors opened. No one was in an ambulance hurry. The crew had time to look about at field and moor and dale and have longings for a farmhouse there and summer all the time. Then one of them came to the front door. Eileen looked from the window and sent him round to the back. 'That's never opened,' she said. She went down to meet the man.

'Now Clare,' said Keith, 'they know what's best.'

'No one knows,' said Clare. And cold ashes from the fireplace were in Keith's hair and down his neck.

There was a friendly ambulance man, and a woman who knew how to do things.

'We'll give you a ride down the stairs,' she said. 'You won't fall out. It's a nice comfy stretcher.'

'I'm comfy here,' said Clare.

'You still will be,' said the woman. 'One, two, three.'

'The one with the black back,' said Clare, changing the subject to pigs. 'Boggy.'

They thought she was swearing. They were not sure what to make of the pigs that were suddenly on the floor under their feet. They did not know what to do about the stretcher that got up from the bed and threw itself out of the window, carefully opening it first.

Clare giggled. Nellie Jack John came stumping up the stairs. 'I've told thee,' he said, 'pigs in t'pig-hoil, not ligging i'bed.'

'They're on the floor,' said Clare.

David thought he could sort things out. 'Now boggart, listen,' he said. 'Side up, and put it all back.'

'No,' said Clare. 'When they've gone back to their hospical.'

The curtains drew themselves across. The electric bulb came out of its socket and broke in the fireplace. Towels floated near the ceiling. The door rattled on its hinges.

'We'll just have a word with the hospital,' said the ambulance man. But when he got to the ambulance the mobile telephone was out of range. And something shut and locked the doors and began to jump on the roof of the vehicle.

186

After a time it was driven away. Bedroom curtains drew themselves back. Pigs were in the own quarters, and ashes were tidily put back quite near the fireplace.

'Hello,' said Clare. 'That didn't take so long.'

XXV

'It never did like me,' said Keith. 'Things don't.'

'You're strange to things,' said David. 'Your jokes are humorous, not wild. You've got good sense and you can be my solicitor. You will never approve of boggarts.'

'No,' said Keith. 'It was disgraceful. I still have ashes in my hair.'

They were eating chips on the way to David's house, hooing and haaing as they burnt their mouths.

'Boggart chips,' said David. 'Burn his mouth.'

At the house Dr Wix caught the smell of chips. 'Where's my bag?' he asked.

'Not for you, Ricky,' said Sister Mackenzie.

'Maybe not,' said Dr Wix. 'Sister and I are just going into town for a meal. The telephone will be switched to Dr Wells's house. If you go out lock up. When you come in leave the latch so I can get in.'

Before the telephone was routed to the other doctor it rang, more or less under Dr Wix's hand. The call was for David.

'Not on the right line,' said Dr Wix.

The wrong line was explained by the caller being Billy.

'Who was that?' she asked. 'Well, I can't speak to him, I'm afraid to. I couldn't get this afternoon and now she isn't in the hospital when I went, and I'm ringing from work so I can't be long, and what's the matter with her?'

'They don't tell me,' said David. 'You'd better talk to him.'

'Does he hate me?' Billy asked.

'Here he is,' said David. 'It's doctor stuff,' he told his father. 'Clare's mother, you know. She doesn't want to speak to you.'

'I'd better speak to her,' said Dr Wix.

'Gently,' said Sister Mackenzie.

'Now, Mrs Rattray,' said Dr Wix. 'Will you listen a moment. I have something to tell you that's not medical at all, but I think you should do it.'

Then he told her what she should do. When he had finished he put the telephone down, and switched calls through to Dr Wells.

'Don't wait up,' he said. 'Be good.' He and Sister Mackenzie went out to the car.

'But will it cure her?' said Keith. 'Is it medical?'

'I don't know,' said David. 'Did it do you any good?'

Martin Malpass told Eileen that any bowl would do. She had polished a silver one, she said, and did it matter about 'Best of Breed, Swaledale Tup, Reeth Show 1912' being written on the side?

'It sounds exactly right,' said Martin Malpass. 'We are all one flock. Is the mother here?'

'She's on the track,' said David. The car with painted flames was picking its way along.

'You don't want tap water,' said Frank. 'It's best from the yard pump.'

'I did the front room out,' said Eileen. 'But I thought the little garden might be better.'

'That would be very nice,' said Martin Malpass. 'Where is the patient?'

'I said it was a cure,' said Keith. 'But I think real medicine would be better. Hospital.'

The patient was upstairs, not sure about what lay ahead. 'If I can wear a shawl,' she said. 'That's what they do.'

Eileen had a shawl. Clare came very slowly down the stairs with it round her head and shoulders.

'Little mite,' said Martin Malpass. 'She can hardly move.'

'She doesn't give up till she tumbles over,' said Frank.

'And here's Sister Mackenzie,' said Keith. He had been looking out for the automatic mountain bicycle and it was now catching up with Billy's car, and then had to wait for it.

'I don't know,' Billy was saying to Martin Malpass. 'It never happened before. Yes, I've heard of them, but I thought they were gangsters.'

'I've looked at them,' said Martin Malpass, 'and they might be. But it's all we've got. So shall we start? I'll use the form of service for the private baptism of infants, commonly called christening, because I'd like you to think seriously about what some of you are undertaking.'

David carried the bowl of water. Nellie Jack John brought along the infant. She had had to stop walking on her own. She had a private arrangement with herself that being carried by Nellie Jack John did not count as being helped.

The garden was quiet. David set the bowl down and Keith heard the water spin round in it. Along the wall-side there was a rustle. He thought it might be a hedgehog.

'Are we all here?' said Martin Malpass. 'Hello, my dear,' he said to Clare. 'Do you understand what is happening?'

'I'd like the pigs done as well,' said Clare.

'Niver did any harm,' said Frank.

'I'm not a vet,' said Martin Malpass. 'Shall we go on?'

This is going to get solemn, Keith thought. Yet we are just people gathered together in a garden.

Then Martin Malpass was talking about gardens, of Eden, and of Gethsemane; and calling forward the godparents.

The godmothers were Eileen and Sister Mackenzie.

'At least two for a girl,' said Martin Malpass. 'And a godfather, of which we have two today.'

Nellie Jack John and Keith were the godfathers.

'Keith is David's friend,' said Clare. 'So that's all right with me.'

'And I were bidden,' said Nellie Jack John. 'Force-put.' But in his grumbling he understood duty.

'Not you, David?' said Martin Malpass.

'I'm something else,' said David. And Nellie Jack John was being put at a distance by being godfather, Keith felt, because David was a possibly true brother to Clare, and Nellie Jack John only in some adoptive way, at best.

Keith knew in the next promisings that they would not be fulfilled – they could not be, but why else would they be made?

'I would like to pick you up,' said Martin Malpass to Clare, 'and pour some water on your head.'

'I can't kneel down,' said Clare. She took off her glasses and gave them to David. 'I can see some things better now.'

'And who will name the child?' said Martin Malpass.

'I will,' said Clare. 'I am Clare. Didn't you know?'

'That's right,' said David.

Clare had water poured on her head, and words were said over her.

'I can hear that kettle whistling,' said Eileen, a few moments later. 'You'll all come in.'

'But this water,' said Martin Malpass, 'is no longer common water. So I don't think the pigs should have it, Frank, but the flowers in this corner will bloom the better.'

He twisted the bowl and the water shot out in a curved sheet, lacy at the edges, and showered some tall yellow stuff transplanted here a month before.

Something else was there too. David saw what it was, though no one else did. It was very upset by the holy water. It spat and hissed, and steam rose from it. It leapt to the top of the wall and began to loosen stones.

'Thou's degged t'boggart wi' howly watter,' said Nellie Jack John. 'By Gow.'

'Boggy,' Clare shrieked, delighted to see him and understanding his state of mind. 'I had a special thing, so don't be naughty.'

'By God indeed,' said Martin Malpass. 'This ought to be dealt with. I can find out about it if you like.'

'No, Vicar,' said Eileen. 'It belongs here. It's ours. Let it alone.'

'I let Keith be a godfather,' said David. 'That needs good solid people like him.'

He doesn't know, thought Keith. He has not understood what is coming. 'Thank you,' he said. 'I'll do my best.' He hoped nothing was best, because there was little more to do.

On their next visit Clare was grumpy. She complained that Muz had not come. 'You said next time,' she told David.

'Next time,' said David. They played cards for a little while, until Clare could no longer hold them, though she understood which of them she meant to play. She and Keith beat David.

When they came again the house was very quiet. Eileen was asleep in a chair by a fallen fire. There was no sound from upstairs. David and Keith went away quietly. There was no more to be done.

'Brought her some chocolate,' said Keith.

They both thought about eating it and did not.

'Next time,' said David.

About a fortnight later, early on a Wednesday afternoon, in a history period dealing with the naval power of the United States from 1807, there was an outdoor noise that seemed somehow in keeping.

Dr Tate, who was manoeuvring the navy, ran his words aground in the Caribbean and went to the window to look.

David found his own eye on Keith. Keith was looking another way, but gradually turned his head to look at David. They knew this sound better than anyone.

By now the whole room was on its feet. It was certain that the noise was coming towards them, and the expectation was proved right. Dr Tate was wrong in looking out of the window.

Nellie Jack John came in at the door. He had traversed the hall and the corridor, beating his call all the way, harried by school secretaries and a large PE instructor. Because of the uniform that he wore they would not touch him. His presence was so real that they considered him an authentic ghost, not an imitation. From that they knew he had a purpose, and let him alone.

'What is it?' said Dr Tate, old-fashioned uniforms running in his mind with the ships he had been discussing.

Nellie Jack John stood in the doorway, rounded off his drumming, and raised his sticks to his chin. Then he dropped them to his sides and stood waiting.

He looked at David and Keith. It was an order.

'We have to go, Sir,' said David. He had no doubt they would.

'My office nine o'clock tomorrow,' said Dr Tate. 'Rest of you sit down. Nothing to discuss.'

Frank was outside the school gates in the Land-Rover. 'He daredn't go in else,' he said. 'Nor me.'

'That's regimentals for thee,' said Nellie Jack John. 'Best get on, then, Frank. Mother will be waiting of us.'

He got into the cab. Keith and David climbed in the back. No one had to tell them anything.

Clare was small in the big bed. She looked at them dreamily.

'She's on her way, is Billy,' said Eileen.

'She wouldn't like to come,' said Clare. 'I'll find her later. Davy.'

'Yes,' said David.

'Muz,' said Clare.

Keith saw David grow small with guilt and look upon himself with shame.

'Next time,' said David. 'Next time.'

'Promise,' said Clare.

'I rushed them out of school,' said Nellie Jack John. 'They'd no time to think. I thowt tha'd want them sooner than owt else.'

'Brother,' said Clare. 'I always knew you were somewhere. What's Eileen doing?'

'Mekking tea,' said Nellie Jack John.

'You'll need that,' said Clare. 'Sit on the edge and I can see you. Nellie, you stand near. Are the pigs too big to come in?'

'Happen,' said Nellie Jack John. 'Porkers, some on 'em.' David sat at one side of the eiderdown, Keith at the other. Nellie Jack John said he would stand guard at the foot of the bed. 'Dressed for it,' he said.

She was still for a time, but her eyes looked from one to another.

'It's dark at the sides,' she said. 'Like that candle.' She brought her hands slowly out from under the covers, then did what she had never done before. She stretched them out to David and Keith. 'Hold them,' she said. 'I might slip over on the way.'

Keith put out his other hand towards David. He was too far and alone to be by himself. David put his hand out too.

Keith for a time thought their hands met, but there was something else there, neither warm nor cold, neither wet nor dry, neither visible nor invisible, waiting on the eiderdown, making an impression.

Clare smiled and sighed. Her hands stayed where they were but no longer held.

After some time Nellie Jack John snapped himself to a hard stance of attention, turned left, took two strides, turned right, came up past Keith, turned and stepped towards the bed beside the pillow.

He removed Clare's glasses with one hand and shut them up. With the other he closed her eyes.

'Gone like a soldier,' he said. 'Our lile scallibrat.'

Last End

'Belike,' Frank had said.

Stones rattled on the garden wall, branches twisted, and all at once the garden flowers were swaying under the rush and scamper of two invisible beings. 'They come from somewhere, after all, and they have to be somewhere, and might have been someone, and laiking in trees is best if you couldn't do it in life.'

One of them fell out of the almond tree. It lay among the flowers for a time, visible only by the way it displaced stems and leaves. It would not be right to reach down and help it.

'You can do it,' said David.

Then it was up the tree again, and walking the tightrope of the top branches and twigs, and leaping to the wall. It had its legs and liberty at last.

'They'll breed,' said Nellie Jack John. 'That's generally what.'

'It isn't the way,' said Frank.

'And,' said Martin Malpass, quietly, 'they were both christened, so they won't. But at the time I wondered whether it had taken, or if it could for both.'

Frank had packed the little casket tight and lifted the turf over it again, pressing it down with his boot.

But it was not necessary. Two other things came and trod the square back into place, its cut edges joining again, the centre of it stretching to a small mound over the little boxes.

'We just do our best,' said Martin Malpass. 'We can't love as much as is necessary, only as much as possible.'

'You get choices,' said David. 'It's hard.'

'You don't,' said Keith. 'It's harder.'

'The kettle will be just at boiling,' said Eileen. 'And scones warm yet. She liked a buttered scone.'

At David's house Kirstie was making a more serious tea; though of course nothing was so seriously large as Eileen's. Nowadays, however, cups and saucers were used, not mugs; not the only change.

'Did it go off well?' she asked.

'Oh yes, Sister,' said David. 'I mean Mum.'

'I just couldna manage it,' said Kirstie. 'Will you hold her while I make the tea.'

She handed over the baby.

'Lyddy,' said David. Elizabeth Clare Wix was her name.

'It was a sad end, and a happy release,' said Kirstie.

Keith remembered waiting afterwards at Swang for Billy to arrive. 'She will have to see to it, I suppose,' Eileen had said. 'Not our business.'

Keith had held a mug of tea with hands that were clammy all the way to his armpits, and a cold tremble across his gut. His forehead felt transparent and empty.

Frank had come in and nodded his head unhappily when he heard how the afternoon had passed. 'I saw she was down,' he said. 'She had that felon all her life.' He meant her sickness and affliction.

Then, when Billy had still not come, he had taken Keith and David to the lane end. They wanted to walk the rest of the way. Keith thought that they might climb up over the hill on the old road above the scar, where they had nearly fallen in the snow.

'She would have been eight next month,' said David. 'Seven is better.'

They had not gone a hundred yards before Dr Wix's Range Rover stopped beside them.

'I'm on a road accident call,' he said. 'Get in. I was up at Thwaite, so I may be too late.' The engine smelt hot.

He was not late enough to matter. A hundred yards further on again, where the road bent to go down the side of Jingle Beck, Constable John Hunter was waiting. He put up a hand that meant, please stop, but not altogether or urgently, because it is too late.

'Sorry, doctor,' he said at the window. 'But there was nothing to be done. Car went off at the other side, went straight on into the gill, into the Cradle, that's its name, the Giants' Cradle, and that was that. The ambulance came and took the driver away. They're looking for the child. She had one, but haven't found it. Maybe it wasn't there.'

Then he had let Dr Wix by, down the slope to the bridge over Jingle Beck, up the other side. And before the road turned away, where the wall was broken, down at the bottom was a smashed blue car that had been in real flames, not the painted ones scorched by reality still showing on the front wing.

That had been months ago. Since then Dr Wix had realised something about Sister Mackenzie.

'What a fool,' he said to David. 'I couldn't see what I was doing, and I daresay all the rest of the world could. I won't ask you to be a bridesmaid, but of course you'll be there.'

'From what I hear,' said David, who had known more than he admitted to Keith, 'I'll be wheeling the pram.'

'It's to be a girl,' said Dr Wix. 'A bit late in some ways, but those are old times. We shan't forget them; but your mother would want us to move on.'

Mr Heseltine, sorting out an old desk in his office, came upon something he showed to Keith in confidence.

'I don't think it should get any further than you and David,' he said. 'But I won't keep it from you. It's about a distant fore-elder of your mother's, quite forgotten about.'

It was an old and thick cutting from a newspaper, yellow and blackened.

It was about a certain John Cherry of Eskeleth, who in 1807 at the age of seventy-three had married a Garebrough woman called Katharine Storcy. He had been forgotten because he had been presumed mad and removed to York, raving about treasure in the hill, and making treasonable assertions about what was to happen in the future. He had left the treasure to the Lord of the Manor, but no one had seen it. With the paper was a very decrepit one pound coin.

'I don't know how that got there,' said Mr Heseltine. 'No one's been in that desk since they brought out pound coins.'

'No problem,' said Keith, looking carefully at the coin. 'But if the date is right it's a forgery for the next twenty-five years.'

Keith went down to St Agatha's with David with some autumn flowers. There were leaves from the trees on the lawn surrounding the gravestone.

'Was I mad?' said David. 'What did I think?'

'All that evidence,' said Keith. 'Names. Muz. Dates.'

'I wish I knew for sure,' said David. 'There's always that possibility.'

'I can sort it out,' said Dr Wix, when Keith took the problem to him disguised as a strained hand. 'Of course I knew what was in his mind. Clare told me. She also told me that while she wanted David as a brother she wouldn't want me as a father, because I was too old. But I thought David couldn't take it seriously. My fault, I expect.

But it was painful for me to fall in love with Kirstie when I had so much loved Elizabeth, and that filled my mind. God knows how many legs I sawed off trying to cure earache, or ears I avulsed instead of ingrown toe-nails. But I'll see to it; I'll make it clear to him, because I can. Meanwhile, for your hand, drink only half pints; full pints will be too heavy to lift.'

'I'm a Methodist,' said Keith. 'We don't.'

'Then use a straw,' said Dr Wix cheerfully.

The next night Keith was at David's house. He was cuddling the baby, which was in a sweet-smelling mood and not even dribbling.

'Do you want to drift away, Keith?' said Dr Wix.

'I'll say goodnight,' said Keith.

'Sit down, you ugly idiot,' said David. 'Hold the baby.'

'There's just a letter I never sent you,' said Dr Wix. 'It might just clear up any doubts. It's still in its envelope, if you want to read it any time.'

'Keith can read it out to me,' said David. 'Give me the baby thing, open it up, the letter not Lyddy, and gas it out, ditto, ditto.'

' "Dear Davy",' Keith read. 'Are you sure?' He had seen the date, not on the postmark because the stamped envelope had not been posted.

'Read,' said David.

'Should I be busy in the kitchen?' asked Kirstie.

'No,' said David.

I have to tell you, Keith went on, *that your dear mother died giving birth to your sister, also dead at birth, tho' a very perfect, whole and pretty baby with hair whom we were to call Clare. This is all I can tell you at present, and I do not know what we shall do next. This is with all my love and grief, Dad.*

'Then that's all right,' said David. 'It's just that it might have been an alien buried at the old church, and now I know it wasn't. And the one that was didn't want to be.'

I was right, thought Keith. I wish I wasn't.

'No aliens at all, in the end,' said David, grinning doubtfully at the baby. 'Unless this suddenly stinky article is one,' and he handed Lyddy over to her mother.

And I was wrong, thought Keith. I wish I wasn't.

'Please have no doubts,' said Kirstie, taking the baby and pulling a face. 'Ricky and I had to think hard about this, though we didn't mention it to each other because it seemed such a worrying big thing. But I was at the Monks' Infirmary then in charge of the ward, and I was on duty, and it was undootedly poor Elizabeth's poor wee dead babe.'

'Much prettier than you were,' said Dr Wix. He was talking to David.

David looked into the baby's eyes. It was quite happy to smell ugly. 'There are too many women in my life,' he said. 'Good.'

At Swang there were some papers to sign.

'Mother,' said Nellie Jack John. 'I can do that. But Dad I'll never get to. It'll ha' to be Frank, whativer.'

'Best get it sorted out,' said Frank. 'I hear the little beggar's courting a lass at Whaw, so happen I'll get Grandpa'd one day soon.' Nellie Jack John looked at him.

They had one of Martha's pigs that night. Frank said too that what was brewed in his dairy wasn't liquor, so a Methodist could drink it.

'I always get sick at Swang,' said Keith afterwards. 'This time it was in the yard, like a boggart in the head.'